She would have to beg  help.

Sawyer Zook! The man who would have been her husband today if she hadn't broken off the engagement.

But for baby Chloe, she needed to focus.

"Please," she begged to not be turned away. "I have a baby."

Sawyer's eyes dropped to the child she held protectively beneath her. The poor child didn't understand what was happening around her. Neither did Naomi, but she did know safety had to be secured quickly, no matter who had to help her.

Sawyer's firm nod said he understood that, too.

"Stay low," he instructed her. "My office is in the back. Get behind the furniture." He nodded at a large bureau with an oval mirror attached. "You go right, and I'll go left. On three. One, two, three!"

The two of them scrambled at the same time, but just as Naomi reached the back of the bureau more gunshots rang out. She managed to get around to the back to meet him there. Another gunshot rang out and glass shattered and rained down on Naomi.

Katy Lee writes suspenseful romances that thrill and inspire. She believes every story should stir and satisfy the reader—from the edge of their seat. A native New Englander, Katy loves to knit warm, woolly things. She enjoys traveling the side roads and exploring the locals' hideaways. A homeschooling mom of three competitive swimmers, Katy often writes from the stands while cheering them on. Visit Katy at katyleebooks.com.

Books by Katy Lee

Love Inspired Suspense

Warning Signs
Grave Danger
Sunken Treasure
Permanent Vacancy
Amish Country Undercover
Amish Sanctuary

Roads to Danger

Silent Night Pursuit
Blindsided
High Speed Holiday

AMISH SANCTUARY

KATY LEE

LOVE INSPIRED SUSPENSE
INSPIRATIONAL ROMANCE

LOVE INSPIRED® SUSPENSE
INSPIRATIONAL ROMANCE

ISBN-13: 978-1-335-40291-2

Recycling programs for this product may not exist in your area.

Amish Sanctuary

This edition published by arrangement with Harlequin Books S.A.

For questions and comments about the quality of this book, please contact us at CustomerService@Harlequin.com.

Love Inspired
22 Adelaide St. West, 40th Floor
Toronto, Ontario M5H 4E3, Canada
www.Harlequin.com

Printed in U.S.A.

And ye shall know the truth,
and the truth shall make you free.
–John 8:32

To my parents, John and Sue. Thank you for everything.

ONE

Racing back to the slow life of the Amish reminded Naomi Kemp of the night she ran away from it. Eight years ago, the one thing that propelled her into the dark unknown of the English world was her own fear. Tonight, it was someone else's that sent her back.

On a frustrated sigh, she flicked the blinker of her small four-door SUV and took the exit off the Kentucky interstate. Ahead, her headlights flashed off the road sign that announced she'd arrived in the small town of Rogues Ridge, home to her Amish roots.

Roots that had been severed by her own hand…and for good reason.

Naomi would never expect a warm welcome from her family—or that certain someone who would have been her husband today. She wouldn't expect forgiveness, but she would expect charity. Just as she had helped a friend in trouble today, she could count on her old community to do the same. They most likely would turn her away, but no one would turn away a child in need of safety.

Would they?

She glanced in the rearview mirror, but not to peer out the back window. The infant car seat behind her held a precious, innocent baby girl just shy of four months old. Chloe Hanover had been entrusted into Naomi's care by a dear friend from her support group. Debby feared for her daughter's safety. The child needed protection, Debby had said. She'd begged Naomi to take Chloe just a few hours ago, asking if she knew of a place they could hide out for a few days until she could fix the situation.

Naomi could think only of one.

Home.

But going home meant facing the people she had hurt the most.

"That's not Chloe's fault." Naomi muttered her thought aloud and followed the old, familiar roads she would know in her sleep. But it wasn't her fault either. At least that was what all that counseling told her. Whether old roads or old patterns of thought, doubts still resided in the deep recesses of her brain, lingering reminders of another time and place and way of life. One where she had been so naive. So trusting.

So blind to the truth.

Bright lights filled the interior of her car's cabin. She flinched at the blaring assault and flipped her mirror up, squinting at the vehicle close behind. Before she could estimate the distance or pull over, a loud bang and crunch shocked her. Naomi gripped the steering wheel with all her might and hit the brakes.

The car hit her!

The tires squealed, but her car continued to career down the road with a high-pitched screech and the stench of burning rubber. The vehicle stayed on hers and pushed her relentlessly from behind. The steering wheel shook in Naomi's hands as the back end of the car slid out under the pressure and curved to the side of the road, nearing a steep embankment.

Loud screams filled the interior over the commotion. Naomi realized both she and the baby were causing them.

"Chloe!" Naomi called out in a panic. The rear right tire breached the road's edge and slipped over it, causing the car to tilt. She screamed louder. She had no way to comfort the child in this moment of terror. She had no way to protect her as the child's mother asked of her. She had no way to stop any of this.

Everything happened so fast. One moment, Naomi had been worrying what her family would say. The next, she feared she would never see them again.

The back end swerved sideways, and the car pushed her from the side. Naomi glanced to her left out her driver's-side window. The hood of the other car was mere inches from her. She peered out into the dark interior of the other car, but could see nothing but the outline of the driver. She made out the brim of a round hat…and maybe glasses.

Too dark to tell.

Too quick to see.

The next second the back tires left the road for the embankment and gravity did its job. Naomi's SUV picked up speed as it fell backward down the drop-off. The uneven and rocky terrain jostled them over every bump and hole, jarring her teeth. All she could do was hold tight to the steering wheel. At another time in her life, she would have prayed. But this night only proved her doubts in a loving God. A loving God wouldn't let bad things happen. She had been wise to turn her back on Him that same night she left her family. Her only justification was He turned away from her first. He let that…that horrible thing happen to her and did nothing to stop it.

She pushed away the long-ago memory of her attack and focused on the child in her care now.

Now God would let this man kill an innocent child.

"I'm sorry, Debby!" Naomi cried out for failing her friend.

Thud.

The car came to an immediate stop, whipping her head back sharply, then forward. Naomi hit the wheel hard on the impact. The SUV must have hit a rock or a tree. Whatever it was, it stopped the car from continuing its descent any farther.

Her focus blurred. She moaned, then realized the baby had stopped crying.

Naomi's heart pounded loud in her chest. Her breathing picked up in a panic. "Chloe?" She whimpered the child's name. Every sound ceased into an unnerving silence. After the loud, tumultuous noises surrounding them moments before, the sound of dead silence instilled more fear in her than anything else.

Tears filled Naomi's eyes at what she would find behind her. *The poor baby.*

Poor Debby.

After all the young mother had been through. She only wanted to give her child a safe life. The child that was innocent in all this.

Would Chloe be the one to pay with her life?

Naomi unclicked her seat belt buckle and prepared for the worst. She used the steering wheel to pull herself forward. The car's position remained on a sharp incline with the hood of the SUV pointing up to the road. As Naomi leaned forward, she froze.

The headlights of the other car glowed dimly and unmoving.

He was still up there!

All Naomi could think was that he wanted to be sure she didn't emerge. Was he waiting for her so he could finish her off? Was this man the trouble Debby feared? All she had said was she thought she had been found. The fear in her eyes was enough for Naomi to go with no questions asked. Now she wished she had demanded answers.

This wasn't a prank to this man. This was a calculated plan to kill.

But who?

Her?

Naomi looked into the dark back seat.

Or the child?

What if he'd already succeeded? Naomi needed to find out.

Slowly, she pushed up onto her knees and turned to face the back. She climbed through the dark car with only the lights from the dashboard and headlights beaming up to the road as her guidance. She left the car running and felt her way, and when she sat in the back seat and faced forward, only then did she reach tentative hands into the rear-facing car seat.

A white blanket covered Chloe. The soft cotton bunched in Naomi's fingers as she pulled it toward her.

Then the blanket pulled back.

Naomi inhaled with a surge of hope. She leaned forward and felt for the baby. She found the hand holding the blanket in a tight grip.

"Chloe?" Naomi whispered.

A gurgle spoke back.

Naomi choked on a surge of grateful tears. Chloe was alive!

But for how long?

The question propelled Naomi into action. That man up there wouldn't wait all night. Soon he would make the trek down to see for himself that his dirty work had been complete.

Naomi felt for the small bag of things she had thrown together. It had been on the seat, but in the impact had been thrown to the floor. Feeling for the zipper of the duffel bag, she opened it and withdrew a long black cloak and black brimmed bonnet.

Making quick work, Naomi soon resembled the young eighteen-year-old she had been the night she left Rogues Ridge. She hadn't donned these clothes since that night and never thought she would again.

She ignored the lingering question about why she kept them and unbuckled the baby. Naomi snuggled the infant inside the cloak. Before opening the door, she leaned forward into the front seat to hit the switch for no interior lights that would alert the man above to her plan.

She would not be going back up the embankment to the road, but rather deeper into the woods. The one thing the man probably didn't plan on was her knowledge of the area. Naomi knew exactly where she would come out on the other side.

Her old best friend's family furniture store.

The idea of seeing Liza Stolzfus again induced a yearning to get a move on. Daylight would be breaking soon. She should arrive just as they were opening. Liza would welcome her with open arms. She would be the only one—but also the only one Naomi could trust.

She stepped out the rear door. She took a few steps around the car and noticed a large boulder had been what kept them from descending farther down the slope. Not God, but a rock.

She made her way down the incline, and just as she reached the tree line, she turned back.

The car lights above still glowed. The man obviously waited for her to come up…or not, because she was dead.

Let him think that, she thought and headed into the trees.

Three steps in, and the sound of a snapping twig from behind halted her. She looked back at the slope up to the road, but all she saw were dark lines of trees amid some rocks.

Then one of the lines had an outline of a circle around it.

No. She pressed her lips and tightened her hold on the baby. Not a circle, but a brim like an Amish hat. However, this one was curved on the sides, like a cowboy hat. The driver had worn a hat, she recalled, but now as she peered closer, she could see the full, tall frame of a man. He stood less than twenty feet away, and she knew the driver had come down the embankment to find her—to finish what he had started.

Naomi did the only thing she could.

She ran.

Sawyer Zook inserted the key into the back door of his furniture shop, Authentic Amish. Handmade craftsmanship at its simplest and finest. It had been four years since he'd taken ownership of the store, and four years since he'd brought the store from servicing local clients to buyers worldwide.

His boots shuffled along the wide-board floors as he closed the private entrance behind him and made his way to his desk. Dropping the keys in the top drawer, he closed it and removed his black wool coat. The pegs on the wall held minimal articles. He placed his coat on a free peg, and as he withdrew his hand, his fingers brushed against the black bonnet hanging from its strings. His *frau* had left it there the last time she worked.

Three years ago.

He turned to start his day just as he had since she'd given him the store after they married. The business had been in her family for generations. As the oldest of three girls, she inherited it and, upon marriage, welcomed him beside her. She had blessed him with such a gift.

It was so much more than he could have asked for. So much more than she got to enjoy. It wasn't fair.

He grimaced at his wayward thought. Bishop Bontrager would scold him for thinking so worldly. It had nothing to do with fairness. God's will would always be done. Even if it meant He took Liza home to be with Him so soon into their marriage.

The back door opened and in walked his apprentice.

"*Gut* morning," Sawyer said to the young man. "Glad you're early. We have a large order to fill."

Caleb Yoder yawned his reply and hung up his coat. "My little *brudder* is teething. He cried all night. Kept the whole house awake. I couldn't wait to get out of there this morning."

Sawyer chuckled but couldn't say he could relate. Liza died before having children. He often wondered what it would have been like if they had *kinner*. Running the business would be near impossible if he had to raise a *boppli* at the same time.

He pushed aside the idea and opened the file of orders his website partner brought over the night before. With his English friend Jim's help, Sawyer had made Authentic Amish a huge success. Sawyer had no time to think about the loss of family when he had so much work to do. His store and all his employees were family enough, despite what his older sister, Anna, kept saying.

A bang from the front of the store echoed through to the backroom, startling them both.

Sawyer glanced at the clock above the doorway. "Too early for customers. The sun's barely up. Stay here and go through these orders. Pick three to work on today. The stack won't be so daunting."

"*Ach*, you might need to hire another employee if these orders keep coming." Caleb sat down to go through the file.

Sawyer left him to his task and wove his way

through the workshop then the store. All the machinery in the workshop ran off diesel with nothing powered by electricity. Even the lights above were powered by gas. It was more efficient than the lanterns he used at his sister's home, where he lived since shortly after Liza's death. He and Liza had lived with her family, and when she became so sick it was best to stay there so they could help. But after she passed, he needed to be with his own family. He was grateful Anna had opened her home to him. She also allotted room in her barn for his woodshop. Now, if he could just convince her he didn't need another wife, all would be peaceful.

Unlike the person banging so relentlessly on his glass storefront door.

As Sawyer made his way through the storefront, he kept the lights off. It allowed him to remain hidden until he could identify the person out so early in the dark of the predawn.

His feet stilled at the sight beyond the glass. It was a woman. The hint of the early sun cresting the ridge far off in the distance gave him the advantage to see her first.

An Amish woman cloaked in black with a black bonnet shielding her face stood outside. Her head was turned over her shoulder, facing the street, so he couldn't make out her identity. But he could tell she cradled something in her arms.

A baby.

Sawyer rolled his eyes to the ceiling. If this was another one of Anna's matchmaking catastrophes, then she had really outdone herself this time. The last girl she'd tried to match him up with had brought him a picnic basket full of fried chicken. It was his favorite, but the skies had opened up and poured on her. He'd sent her home out of mercy.

Did Anna think he wouldn't turn away a woman with a baby?

Sawyer sighed and resolved himself to the conversation ahead and went to turn the lock. As soon as he did, the woman pushed through in a rush and barreled inside.

"I need help." She looked over her shoulder frantically. "I'm a friend of Liza's. Is she here?"

"A friend of *Liza's*?" Irritation threaded his voice. How dare this woman ask for his wife? She was no friend. A friend would know. She would have been at Liza's vigil, which had lasted for three days. He withheld his retort and asked, "How do you know Liza?"

"Please, there's no time. Someone's chasing me."

Sawyer reached for the light switch.

"No!" she shouted, still glancing over her shoulder. "Don't turn it on. He'll see I'm here."

"And just who are you? And how do you know Liza?"

"We're good friends," the woman said, dropping her head down in a shake. She spoke breathlessly in a rush, saying, "I mean, we were friends. The best of friends. I've been gone for a long time. My name is Naomi Kemp. I grew up in Rogues Ridge. Please, won't you help me?"

Sawyer shrank back.

Naomi Kemp? It couldn't be.

His throat tightened and he could only sputter at the information just thrown at him. He denied such a thing, and in the next second, flipped the light switch to see for himself.

"I said no, don't do that!" she cried with pure fear in her voice, dropping to the floor in a crouch.

The next second, the glass of his front window shattered into a million pieces, and the wall beside him splintered with a hole at the center.

Right where the woman had been standing a moment before.

"Get down!" she yelled and pulled at his pant leg while covering the infant with her bent head. "Now! Or you'll be shot."

Shot?

The idea was unfathomable. And yet, the bullet lodged in his wall proved otherwise.

In a daze, he followed the woman's orders and knelt in front of her. There he came face-to-face with Naomi Kemp.

"It really is you." Stunned, his breathing halted.

Her eyes widened from beneath the bonnet. "Sawyer?" she whispered. Her own shock was apparent. Her mouth fell wide. She swallowed hard before saying, "What are you doing here?"

Instant anger flared, and before he could hold his tongue, he said to the woman he once asked to marry, "You'll be the only one answering that question today. Right after you explain why someone is shooting at you."

TWO

Naomi stared into the one pair of blue eyes she had hoped she would never have to face again. How could they be the first pair she looked into upon her return? Clearly it was all the proof she needed that she should have never returned. If being run off the road, chased through the woods by a mad man, then shot at wasn't enough.

Now she had to beg Sawyer Zook for help.

Sawyer Zook!

The man who would be her husband today if she hadn't left town after that horrifying night at the Englishers' high school party. She hadn't thought she could ever face him again, except here he was mere inches away, and all she could do was hope he had never found out about that night. The only other person who knew, besides her attacker, had promised her he wouldn't tell. Was her secret still safe? Or did the whole town know by now?

Naomi forced her attention from that horrid thought and focused on the danger at hand. She glanced down at Chloe. She needed to focus on safety for the baby, and safety alone.

She humbled herself and begged to not be turned away. "Please. I have a baby."

Sawyer's eyes dropped to the child she held protectively beneath her. Chloe stirred and whimpered with a fearful expression. The poor child didn't understand what was happening. Neither did Naomi, but she did know safety had to be secured quickly, no matter who had to help her.

Sawyer's firm nod said he understood that too.

"Let me take—"

At his pause, she quickly replied, "Her. Her name is Chloe Han…" Naomi stumbled at giving the child's full name. She sought help, but she couldn't be sure who she could trust completely. Thankfully, Sawyer didn't notice as he reached for the infant and gently tucked her into the crook of his arm. The baby looked so much smaller against his wide, tall frame. There was so much more of him than she remembered from their youth. Holding Chloe close and secure as he was, she had the sense that he could take on the world.

"Stay low," he instructed her. "My office is in the back. Get behind the furniture." He nodded at a large bureau with an oval mirror attached. "You go right, and I'll go left. On three. One, two, three!"

The two of them scrambled at the same time, but just as Naomi reached the back of the bureau more gunshots rang out. She managed to get around to the back to meet him there. Another gunshot rang out and glass shattered and rained down on Naomi.

She screamed and covered her head as she realized

the bullet hit the mirror. "Why are there mirrors in an Amish store?" she yelled and pushed up to cover the baby.

But Sawyer turned Chloe away quickly. He wrapped his other arm around Naomi and pulled her close. "Stay low, I said!" His large body over her felt impenetrable, but she knew no matter how strong and muscular he was, he was no match for a bullet.

Naomi's cheek pressed against his chest, feeling his erratic breathing. Surprisingly, she felt protected. The idea was ludicrous, but for the moment, it gave her strength. "What next?" she asked, lifting her face from his blue cotton shirt and brushing against his collar-length brown hair.

He bent his head down, their faces closer than before. So close she could feel his warm, quick breaths and smell coffee from his lips. Their gazes locked, his blue and hers brown. Eyes that used to hold love and tenderness for each other now held fear and confusion.

He shook his head. "I don't know. All I do know is I won't let go of you. I promise."

Naomi inhaled sharply at his straightforward declaration. Why would he say such a thing?

His head turned to look at something behind him. "There's an entertainment center tall enough to protect us." He looked back down at her. "This time, I'll be right behind you."

Tears pricked Naomi's eyes. They were the words she had hoped for when she left eight years ago. All the lonely days and nights, alone in the city of Louisville and out of her element, she had dreamed he'd be right behind her, that he would come for her and would have followed her anywhere.

"You'll be all right," he said and looked to Chloe. "Your baby will be too."

Naomi frowned. She needed to tell him she wasn't Chloe's mother.

"Stay low. Are you ready?" He leaned away from her and nodded at the entertainment center. "Go!"

Naomi did as he instructed, running on her knees and hands, and crouched over. She felt Sawyer close on her heels, then coming up alongside her, ushering her forward and protecting her body with his.

They reached the tall cabinet and pressed their backs against it. From there, Naomi could see into the office door beyond the machinery in the workshop.

Something moved behind the door frame.

"Sawyer, someone's in your office," she whispered frantically.

"I know. It's my apprentice. I hope he called the sheriff's office."

"Do you have a phone in there?"

"Yes, for business purposes, I can have one." He leaned over to peer on the other side of the cabinet. "It's quiet. I think the shooter has left. Who is he? How do you know him?"

"I don't. I was helping a friend who thought she was being followed. Next thing I know, I'm being targeted. He ran me off the interstate. Then he chased us through the woods. I lost him a while back, but when I entered downtown, I saw a car moving slowly. It must have been him looking for me. I knew if I could just get to Liza, she would help."

Sawyer jerked his head back at her. "Liza's dead."

Nothing could have hit Naomi harder than the news that her lifelong childhood friend was no longer on this earth. "Wh-when?" Her voice squeaked, and she covered her mouth.

"Three years ago."

Naomi looked at Sawyer, expecting to see compassion from him. Instead, anger darkened his blue eyes to gray. Her hand fell from her mouth at the sight she had never seen in him in all their childhood.

He had changed.

"You would have known that if you had stuck around." His words were like daggers. "Just because you didn't want me didn't mean you had to hurt everybody else who loved you." He looked over his shoulder. "Caleb! Call Sheriff Shaw!"

Naomi jolted at his deep command to his apprentice. She then trembled as his cruel words echoed in her head. He was so far off the mark, but there was nothing she could say to right his thinking. To do so would mean telling the truth of why she'd really left town. And that wasn't possible. Sharing her story in the support group was one thing. Those people didn't know her. She wouldn't have to see them in the outside world. She wouldn't have to face them, knowing they knew her secret.

"They're on their way," the apprentice called out, a young boy by the sound of trepidation in his cracking voice. "Is it safe?"

"Not yet. Stay there," Sawyer ordered. "And make sure the rear entrance is locked."

"I already did."

"Well done, Caleb."

Sirens sounded off in the distance. Help was on the way.

"I'm sorry I hurt everyone," Naomi whispered. "I never wanted to." She shook her head, unable to say more. To see his disgust for her would be so much worse than his anger. She held on to that consolation. "And I'm sorry I wasn't here for Liza. I want to tell her husband how sorry I am. Who did she marry?"

Sawyer's eyes dimmed back to their light blue. His lips twisted a bit but before he could speak, the sound of glass crunching in the front of the store stopped him.

"Sheriff's department!" a woman's deep voice bellowed. "Is everyone safe? The ambulance is on the way if there are injuries."

Sawyer lifted his face and yelled, "We're safe, Sheriff Shaw. No one's been hurt." He eyed Naomi and whispered, "Today."

Naomi dropped her gaze to her hands in her lap, where they wrung together tightly. She let them go to reach for Chloe, but withheld eye contact from Sawyer. Thankfully he passed the baby over to her. "I meant what I said. I want to apologize to Liza's husband." Naomi fussed with the baby's coat collar.

"Don't bother," Sawyer said and stood up.

"Please tell me who he is." Naomi implored him to give her this opportunity to fix a wrong.

His smirk was back as he looked down at her. Just as he turned to step out from behind the cabinet, he said, "Me, Naomi. Liza married *me*."

Minutes ticked by. Somewhere in the room Sawyer was talking to the officers, but the words reached

Naomi's ears in a contorted muffle. Her chest ached, and she pulled the baby close to her and forced herself to take a ragged breath. She pressed her cheek to the top of Chloe's soft head of satiny auburn hair. The texture should have comforted Naomi, but with Sawyer's announcement bouncing around in her mind, she couldn't feel a thing. All she knew was she had been wrong about the impact of learning about Liza's death. She had thought nothing could have taken her down faster than that.

Thoughts tried to form into words.

Liza, her best friend.

Sawyer.

Her Sawyer.

Married?

Suddenly, all Naomi wanted was to run from this place again. Slowly, she stood and tucked Chloe beneath her cloak. The office door beckoned. A glance around the cabinet showed Sawyer intently discussing the shooting. With her head bent and face shielded by the brim of her bonnet, she moved her feet toward the exit.

She passed by various woodshop machines, cutting in and out around them quickly. A few more steps, and she would be through the door and out the back exit Sawyer had mentioned to Caleb.

She took two more steps, then halted. Or rather, was halted. She turned her head to see a hand on her shoulder.

"Running away again?" Sawyer chided her from behind. "I'm sorry, but this time, you're not going anywhere."

THREE

"Do you have any idea why this man came after you?" Sheriff Cassie Shaw asked Naomi. The two sat alone in Sawyer's office while the rest of her team processed the scene out in the storefront and on the street. Sawyer had been with them, until the sheriff had asked him to leave. "We're alone now, if that will help you speak freely."

Naomi nodded once. Somehow the woman understood Naomi's hesitancy to share with Sawyer in the room. If there had been any question of whether he could be trusted before, now she had her answer.

Sawyer Zook considered her the threat, and that meant she could trust no one. Possibly not even the law.

She tested the waters and said, "I run a support group for women who have experienced certain...traumas."

"'Certain traumas'? As in assault?" Sheriff Shaw glanced at Chloe in Naomi's arms.

Naomi dropped her gaze to the sleeping baby snuggled so peacefully, oblivious to the danger she'd been through tonight, and even the dangerous way she'd come into this world to begin with.

Naomi looked back at the sheriff. "I became close to

one of the women in the group, and she moved in with me recently. She had no one to turn to after her attack, and she feared she was being stalked by him again. I didn't believe her. I didn't think it was possible, but she suggested I take Chloe somewhere safe until she could figure out if the threat was real."

"Why wouldn't it be possible?" Cassie Shaw tilted her slim jawline up. Her black hair was pulled back tight into a low bun. Her light green uniform shirt was clean and crisp. She was a no-nonsense officer, and Naomi sensed she would be thorough. But would she care? The last sheriff Naomi remembered from Rogues Ridge had never seemed approachable, but that could have been Naomi's Amish upbringing of avoiding the English law enforcement—even the night of her own assault. Besides, it wasn't like she was left to handle the situation alone. She had help from a nice stranger that night. A man named James Clark had found her in her distress, and he understood her need to forget that night forever. It was not a night she ever wanted to face again.

She shifted in her ladder-back chair and replied, "I guess I should say I hoped it couldn't be possible. The idea of a second attack…" Naomi swallowed hard and closed her eyes to regroup her wandering thoughts heading into the dark places of her memory. Another event from last year came to mind. She opened her eyes in a flash and blurted out, "There was a death last year. A woman in my group died when she was hit by a car. It was a hit-and-run, but what if… No, that's absurd. The idea of being attacked by the same person is not helping me to think clearly." She gulped and lifted her chin. "Is it typical for a rapist to target the same victim again? Does that happen a lot?" Naomi swallowed her own fear at the horrid idea. It was too much to imagine.

Cassie studied Naomi while she twirled her pen between her fingers. "It's probably just a coincidence. I'm sure you don't have anything to worry about, Naomi."

Her words were meant to calm Naomi. As hard as she tried to cover up her fear, Cassie was sure to see right through her.

"You think this guy tonight could be unrelated to anyone's assault then?" Hope filled her voice.

The sheriff cleared her throat and pursed her lips. "You really don't know who drove you off the road and shot at you?"

Naomi shook her head. "All I can guess is it has something to do with Debby since she felt someone was following her."

"Had your friend ever told you the identity of her attacker?"

"It's confidential, what we talk about in group. Sometimes we share names, but she never mentioned his name. At least not in any session."

"But you know," Cassie raised her eyebrows.

"I do have some idea of his name, but I could be wrong. She talks in her sleep, so it's really a guess."

Cassie let out a frustrated sigh and Naomi knew this was not a lead she could work with.

"All right then, can you tell me your friend's name?" the sheriff asked her. "If for no other reason than so I can contact the local force in Louisville and have an officer do a wellness check."

A wave of relief swept over Naomi. She provided

the address, saying, "I appreciate you doing this. Her full name is Debby Hanover."

The pen made a scratching sound as the sheriff took notes. "Is she married?" she asked as she wrote.

Naomi shook her head, then Cassie continued. "When was she assaulted?"

Naomi looked down at Chloe before giving her reply. "A little over a year ago."

"And how about yourself? Are you—"

Naomi lifted her chin in a flash. "My past really isn't important here."

Cassie widened her eyes, then frowned. "Sorry, I was asking if you're married."

The door opened, and in walked Sawyer and one of the deputies.

Naomi held her response, but Sawyer said, "Go ahead and answer the question. I was actually wondering the same thing. Are you married?"

Naomi felt her head swirl in instant light-headedness. Sawyer had heard the sheriff's question through the door. What else had he heard? She tried to think if she'd said anything about her last night in this town.

His pointed stare wasn't filled with revulsion or discomfort. The fact that he looked her in the eye proved her secret was safe from him…so far. She would rather he spend the rest of his life hating her than knowing about that horrid night.

"Sawyer," Sheriff Shaw interrupted, "I think it's best if I ask the questions in private."

"I'm fine," Naomi said. "I'll answer your questions about Debby honestly and openly. I came here for protection from a dangerous man. I want to know who he is and why he tried to kill me." She looked up at Sawyer in the doorway. "But if you must know, I'm not married. And I never was." *Unlike you, who married my best friend.*

She gave him two seconds to drop his questioning gaze to Chloe and ask how she came to be when there was no husband in the picture.

Sawyer did it in one, though his question was unspoken. She saw it in his eyes as he looked back to her.

"How about a boyfriend?" Sheriff Shaw asked. "Or an ex-boyfriend you might have…a problem with."

Naomi knew this whole scene painted her in a sordid light, but she shook her head. "There's no one in my life. I am not the one in danger here. Debby is." Naomi hoped they would leave it at that. Until she heard from Debby, she needed to protect the child. Her friend was adamant about keeping the baby's identity a secret. "Can you please contact the Louisville Police Department and have them check on her? Then we can go from there."

Sheriff Shaw paused, but acquiesced and called for a deputy to follow up with the address Naomi had given her. Once the man left the room, she turned back to Naomi and said, "You say you aren't the one in danger, but the events that transpired here tonight say otherwise. I need to follow all avenues and search under every rock. It's for your and Chloe's safety. Someone tried to kill you both. Your cooperation will help me figure out who. My job isn't to figure out the why, so all I need are the facts. No personal details. Just the people in your life who may have ill will toward you."

Naomi glanced Sawyer's way. She wondered if she should start with him.

As she faced Sheriff Shaw again, her gaze passed over something on the top of a wooden filing cabinet. A double take still left her dumbstruck.

A laptop in an Amish store?

It was the third time she thought something was off in this place. A mirror, an entertainment center and now a laptop.

Phones were allowed for businesses, but Naomi didn't think computers were. She'd been gone for eight years, but she didn't think that acceptance would ever happen. Even if fifty years had gone by.

Something strange was going on with Sawyer. For a quick second, she wondered if he had a car too. Maybe he was the one who'd pushed her off the road after all. She had seen a tall man with a brimmed hat. Sawyer's hat hung right behind Sheriff Shaw's hat on the pegs. But the driver's hat had been more of a cowboy hat. And he had a handgun.

Would Sawyer own a gun?

Naomi dismissed such a notion as impossible. A handgun would cross the line. Plus, it had been Sawyer dodging the bullets and covering her to protect her and Chloe. He wasn't the shooter.

And he wasn't the man who'd pushed her off the road.

With her pen at the ready again, Cassie asked, "Anyone who has harmed you in the past."

Keith.

Naomi felt her heartbeat skip at the only name she could give. That was all she knew of him, and maybe that wasn't even a real name. Maybe he had made it up to cover his true identity. But the other people at the party called him by that name. They all would have needed to have been involved in his sick and dangerous plan.

She swallowed hard at the idea of writing up that list of names. It was impossible. Plus, there was no reason to include any of them, including Keith. That was so long ago, and he couldn't hurt her anymore. Thanks to the kind man who'd helped her, she moved on to another life, safe and free from that kind of danger.

"I left the Amish community, but aside from my counseling job at the clinic, I never really left the Amish lifestyle. I don't even own a television. I keep to myself and live simply. I don't involve myself in the ways of the English, so I can't see how I can make enemies of them. I'm not even registered to vote." It was the best way she could respond to Sheriff Shaw's question. "I'm glad I can't give you a list of people who would harm me. If there was anyone, I would tell you, but there's not. There is no one in my life now, and there hasn't been since…since I left Rogues Ridge."

Chloe stirred awake and let out a cry. The piercing sound increased to an earsplitting crescendo that had Naomi jumping up to pace with her. "Shhhh," she whispered against Chloe's soft auburn wisps of hair. Naomi bounced her a bit, but to no avail.

"She's probably hungry," Sawyer said.

"Hungry?" Naomi paused midbounce. "Right, of course. She's gone all night."

Sheriff Shaw stood. "We can leave you some privacy

to feed her. I'll be right out in the store when you're ready to continue."

Privacy? Naomi bit her lower lip. "Um, actually, she takes formula, but…" Naomi cleared her throat, realizing she didn't have the baby's bag of necessities. She spoke over the cries. "I left the bag in the car."

Sheriff Shaw looked to Sawyer quickly, then jumped into action. "I'll head over to the supermarket to grab some essentials. Be right back. Don't leave here unprotected."

Cassie Shaw bypassed Sawyer for the door and disappeared through it on her mission. Sawyer stayed put watching Naomi do her best to soothe the hungry baby—a baby that was pushing her away in her distress. Chloe wanted only one person, and that was her mother.

Nothing Naomi did calmed the baby. Nothing she said brought comfort. Sawyer stood by watching with a perplexed expression. Then he stepped up to take her. Naomi stared at his open arms but didn't relinquish the crying baby.

Then he spoke.

His voice sounded different. Softer and endearing. He soothed not only Naomi, but even Chloe paused in her wailing to take notice.

Slowly, Naomi put the baby into his hands and watched him prop her up on his wide shoulder. He nestled her head by his neck, all the while murmuring comforting words and promises.

"All will be well. You're safe, little one. All your cares will be met."

Naomi closed her eyes, wishing his promises were meant for her. She let every word fall over her and bring her peace. When the baby's cries dimmed to discomforted whimpers, Naomi opened her eyes to find Sawyer watching her.

She forced a smile. "You're better at that than I am."

He didn't return the smile, but instead said, "I noticed."

Sawyer watched Naomi place Chloe into the Amish cradle he had on display in the store. The scooped sides and slats around the top had been carved and sanded by his own hand, but never had he imagined while he smoothed and polished the piece to a satiny finish that it would be Naomi placing her child into it.

She leaned over the side and kissed the contented child, brushing a curved finger along her chubby cheek before standing back up and searching the room for Cassie Shaw.

"She's a happy baby again. Thank you for running to the store for the supplies," Naomi told the sheriff. "Have you heard anything about Debby yet?"

Cassie shook her head. "I expect to any minute. But for now, shall we continue our discussion?"

Naomi quickly glanced Sawyer's way. She looked back at Cassie and shrugged uneasily. "I've told you everything."

Cassie sighed. "All right, how about we go about this differently? Is there any way the father of Chloe is the man who pushed you off the road?"

Naomi inhaled sharply. Her gaze flitted from Cassie to Sawyer, and he thought she turned green right in front of them. He would have to say Cassie had hit on a sensitive spot. Naomi's delay in responding and the fear he saw growing in her eyes nearly had him telling her not to worry about answering, but how would that help the police catch this guy?

"There's no judgment here, Naomi," Cassie assured her. "We want to help you."

"It's not that," Naomi said and looked down at the sleeping baby. "She's innocent in all this."

"So is that a yes?" Cassie asked. "Chloe's father could be the one coming after you?"

Naomi sighed, but nodded her answer. She looked to Sawyer and quickly dropped her gaze back to the baby.

Just then, Cassie's cell phone rang into the uncomfortable silence. She reached for it on her belt and looked at the screen. "Something to consider is putting Chloe into protective custody. It may be the safest thing for her until we have a lead. Excuse me, I'll be right back. This is the call I've been waiting for."

As Cassie walked away to take the call, Sawyer moved up to the cradle. He stood on the opposite side, facing Naomi.

"Protective custody?" Her voice squeaked, and her breathing picked up. She shook her head. "I made a promise to take care of her. I can't be separated from her."

"And you won't be," he replied, placing a hand on the cradle's edge. He had no idea why he would assure her of such a thing. It was crazy to involve himself in Naomi Kemp's problems, but her obvious distress reached down deep inside him and dragged out his old need to protect her.

And now her child.

Naomi watched Cassie across the room. "You heard the sheriff. Chloe is safer with someone else besides me." Pain flashed in her eyes. Sawyer gripped the bed-rail tighter. The direction of his thoughts shocked him into silence. The plan forming in his mind had to be denied. He watched Naomi drop her head in a sign of defeat. "Maybe she's right."

"Don't say that," he said. He'd witnessed her struggle with calming the baby in the office, but that didn't mean she wasn't a good mother. It didn't mean she should let someone else take the child.

Not when he had a perfectly good home that was secluded from the English world.

The idea was crazy. And yet, he wanted to know what she thought. She probably wouldn't even accept such a convoluted offer. Nor should she. At least one of them would be acting responsibly.

Sawyer let the idea go for a more realistic plan.

Naomi had yet to look up at him, but he would talk to the top of her pale blond head of curls if he had to. "You've been through more than I can imagine. I know it's been a long night, but it's important to tell the police the details so they can catch this guy. Unless you don't want them catching him?"

Naomi now faced him straight on. "Of course I want them to catch him. He nearly killed us." She pointed to Chloe. "He has to be caught."

"Then who is he?"

Naomi's lips trembled. "I wish I knew."

"You don't know the father of your baby?" Sawyer asked in confusion.

Naomi closed her eyes on a sigh. "She's not—"

"Excuse me," Cassie stepped up to the cradle, stopping Naomi from answering his question. She stood at the bottom with the face of a bad-news bearer. "I'm sorry to tell you this, but an officer was sent out to your apartment. Debby's body was found. It appears she was strangled."

Sawyer watched Naomi's fingers curl around the railing of the cradle. She fisted them tight as though to hold on for dear life. When she began to crumple to the floor, he moved just in time to catch her before her knees gave out.

He wrapped both arms around her and pulled her close to his chest, turning her to cup her head as she trembled uncontrollably over this unfathomable news. His own body reacted automatically and shook, as well. Whoever this Debby was, her life had been cut short at the hands of a killer. He didn't want that for anyone.

"I'm so sorry about your friend," he whispered against Naomi's soft curls, realizing it could have been her. "If you hadn't left…" His voice trailed off, unable to say what could have happened to her, along with her friend.

Cassie cleared her throat. "Debby was murdered, and whoever did this has already tracked Naomi down to be next. We need to address the fact that this killer nearly succeeded in a triple homicide today," she said. "You're not safe out in the open, Naomi. I need to arrange a place of safety for you. And for Chloe. I can arrange for the child services to come today."

"No." Sawyer gripped Naomi's cotton blouse with no inclination of letting go. His previous plan jumped to life again. "She'll be safe with me. They both will.

No one will find them at the farm. The house is in my brother-in-law's name and not connected to the store at all. Even if the killer tries to track me down, he won't be able to. It's secluded, and they'll be protected. I'll make sure of it."

Cassie paused to consider the option. After a moment, she gave a short nod, but looked to Naomi and asked, "Are you all right with that arrangement, Naomi? I can tell the two of you have some history."

Naomi sniffed loudly, then lifted her head. She met Sawyer's eyes straight on, filled with a deep well of questions and uncertainty. He expected her to scoff at his offer.

Maybe she would run away again like she did the last time he made an offer to her.

Her chin trembled as she lifted it high. "I came back here because I knew it would be the safest place to hide. I didn't dare hope anyone from my community would help me, but I'd hoped someone would help Chloe. Thank you, Sawyer, for your willingness to help us both. I accept your offer of protection, even though I know it won't be easy."

He let out a short laugh. Another person came to mind who might stop this plan of action in its tracks. "That is certain sure. Just so you know, you may be running again when my sister sees you coming." He shook his head on a sigh. "You haven't seen Anna's wrath yet. But I'll explain to her this is only for charity." He looked straight at her, needing her to see the warning in his eyes, and said, "Because it is."

FOUR

Anna Miller and her husband Esau lived on a vast farm on the outskirts of town. Multiple barns dotted the rolling green landscape, and two large white homes overlooked the thriving property. Naomi sat beside Sawyer atop his buggy as he drove the chestnut mare down the long, winding lane. They passed by horses grazing behind a long white fence that lined the drive. Cows dotted the pasture in the hills, and corn had recently broken through the rich soil.

"I assume this is Esau Miller's family's property?" Naomi asked.

"*Ya*, the *daudihaus* is the one on the far hill. Esau's parents have a separate drive and use the barn in the middle for their personal animals."

"Why do you live here?" Naomi quickly pressed her lips tight when the question spilled out. "I'm sorry, I didn't mean to pry."

Sawyer shrugged and drove the buggy toward an enormous red barn with its double doors wide. A tall silo sat behind, connected to a long milking shed. Everything was pristine and well cared for, with ample amounts of space. "My parents had another baby after you moved. I'm no longer the youngest male, so their farm will go to little Peter. It's just as well. I'm more of a carpenter than a farmer. When I married Liza, we took over the furniture business and lived with her family until…" He cleared his throat. "My sister offered me a room soon after. It's worked out for everyone, I think."

Naomi nodded solemnly, although the words *worked out for everyone* sounded more like a sacrifice on his part. Where was his family? Where was his own place to call home?

He eyed her. "I see what you're thinking, and don't. The business is enough for me. I'm able to devote all my time to making it a successful venture. I've taken it so much further than Liza's *daed*. I have so many plans for it in the future. Just you wait and see." He smiled bright and flicked the reins to bring the buggy up to the barn doors.

Naomi liked seeing the spark of excitement in Sawyer's eyes, but just as fast as it came, it vanished.

As they reached the opening, he glanced back at the sprawling farmhouse, then turned a stern expression on her. "We need to discuss what to expect under Esau's roof. He likes order." Sawyer's warning felt personal.

"And you think I will bring chaos into their home? What would give you that idea?"

"I don't think you'll have to do anything to create chaos." He drove the horse the rest of the way inside and locked the brakes. Then he glanced down at Chloe asleep in Naomi's arms and said, "It's just bound to happen when they see you."

Naomi tightened her hold on the infant. "I can only be here if it's safe for Chloe. If you don't think—"

Chloe stirred awake and let out a cry, cutting Naomi off. The baby struggled to pull away, wanting someone else entirely.

Naomi squeezed back the tears threatening to spill. This poor child would never see her mother again. And there was nothing Naomi could say to help her understand. "It's all right, Chloe." She whispered the faint words of comfort, even though things were not all right, and they never would be again for the little girl, who was now orphaned. "I'll keep you safe. I promise," she whispered over the discomfited baby.

Sawyer stepped down from the buggy. "Here, let me take her so you can climb down." He held his arms up.

Chloe lifted her own pudgy arms out for Sawyer, straining toward him.

Naomi passed Chloe down. "Looks like she favors you."

"*Nein*, she favors her *mudder*. She just knows she's in a strange place, that's all. I'm certain sure she will settle down soon, once she becomes familiar with her surroundings."

Naomi dropped her gaze to pick up the bag of baby items Sheriff Shaw had purchased. She busied herself as she mumbled, "*Ya*, she does favor her *mamm*." It was the truth, even if Sawyer didn't know Debby was Chloe's mom.

With the bag in her hand, she stood and watched Sawyer offer an outstretched hand to assist her. He had Chloe securely positioned over one shoulder, which freed up his other hand to help her too. His natural capabilities to handle a baby and do something else at the same time didn't go unnoticed. Was he trying to show her he knew she wasn't the baby's mother?

She pursed her lips and said, "I think I remember how to get down off the buggy." Her flare of annoyance came through her every word.

His eyebrows shot up. A slow smirk grew with a dare in his eyes. "A lot can change in eight years. It will be interesting to see how you fare. Especially if you continue to handle the weight of it all alone." His gaze grew serious and held hers.

Did he know?

Naomi prepared to admit the truth right then and there, but her throat grew dry and the words echoed around her mind instead of forming on her tongue. A battle ensued within her.

"I just don't want to put more people at risk." The excuse sounded lame to her own ears.

"Why? Is your friend dead because of you?"

His question hit her straight on.

"I—I don't think so, but…" Her eyes closed on a brief sigh. It was a possibility. She helped a lot of women and knew many of their attackers by name. She couldn't tell Sawyer what she did for a living. To do so would mean opening up on a topic that wasn't a possible discussion. Behind her eyelids, she pictured the look on his face if he found out she had once been one of those women.

She opened her eyes wide in a flash, shaking her head profusely. *No way.*

"Fine, have it your way," he said and stepped back to let her climb down on her own. The message was clear that his lack of assistance would exceed past helping her from a buggy.

It was for the best, Naomi thought. There was no need to depend on him. As soon as the police found Debby's killer, she would go back to her life in Louisville. Until then, she felt safe here hiding out on the farm. Knowing how private the Amish were, she figured she could stay here forever and never be found.

She grimaced at the thought. Forever wasn't an option.

Sawyer went to the front of the buggy and removed a black rectangular case. It dawned on her what it held.

"You brought your laptop with you?"

"I had to if I'm going to be working from my workshop here. My website tech will be in periodically and will need it. Don't worry, it will stay in the barn. No technology or electricity in the house. I know the rules." He walked over to a door and opened it.

Following, Naomi saw a long room filled with machinery. At a desk in the far corner, Sawyer put the laptop down and came back out. Chloe had settled back into a deep sleep on his shoulder. He carried her so comfortably it made her wonder how he had come to know how to handle babies.

Suddenly, Naomi wondered if he and Liza had children. He hadn't mentioned it, but he also hadn't said they hadn't. Was she about to meet a little Sawyer or Liza running around? Naomi's breathing tightened in preparation. The idea bothered her to the point that she prepared to force a smile. She would show kindness even in the midst of the betrayal she felt from them. She felt betrayed by her best friend for marrying the man she had been engaged to. It was a good-size community and many other Amish communities lived around them. Liza could have married someone else. Why had she married Sawyer?

"Komm," Sawyer said, leading her out of his office. "I'll show you the spare room you can use."

Naomi's throat dried in an instant. The idea of staying under the same roof as Sawyer just became a reality. She looked up as he closed the door behind them. At the far end of the barn was a ladder that led to a loft.

She licked her lips as her mind raced. "I could just stay out here in the loft. I don't want to disrupt your sister's home."

"Don't be ridiculous."

"I've stayed in many lofts growing up."

"Well, you've grown up, and you have a baby. So those days are over." Sawyer disregarded her plight and turned toward the barn doors. At the opening he stopped and looked over Chloe's head, nestled against his neck so perfectly. He frowned when he saw Naomi hadn't moved one step. "I can't protect you if you're out here, Naomi. Think of Chloe if something happens to you."

Her gut clenched. The child would have no one.

On a sigh, Naomi nodded and followed her ex-fiancé out of the barn and to his home. "I'm not Amish anymore," she said when they walked in slow steps. The large house loomed ahead of them with the unknown behind the screen door. "Will I be shunned?"

Sawyer walked a few steps without an answer. Then he said, "You were never baptized in the church. Shunning isn't a possibility."

"But rejection is." She looked pointedly at the side of his face, wishing he would look at her.

"The Amish are forgiving people. You know this. You will be welcomed here."

Naomi squeezed her fists tight on the shopping bag. They were nearly at the foot of the porch steps. "You're not being realistic, Sawyer. You just keep walking toward that door as though we do this every day. Are you even considering how frightening this is for me? I know people around here have not thought kindly of me for the past eight years. Including yourself."

He stopped.

Naomi halted, her sneakers sliding in the dirt. She waited for him to say something, but he just looked to the house. With his gaze fixed dead ahead, Naomi followed to see what he looked at.

Anna stood behind the screen door, her hand paused on the handle. Brother and sister squared off while Naomi's heart rate sped up and pounded through her head.

Anna's heated stare told Naomi all she needed to know. "The loft is still an option," she mumbled under her breath.

"*Hullo*, Anna," Sawyer said calmly. "I'm sure you've heard about the shooting in town. We're going to have a couple houseguests until the man is caught. I'm sure you understand, *ya*?"

Anna pressed her lips firmly. After a long moment, she slowly nodded and pushed the screen wide. She stepped out to hold the door open for them with her back. Her arms went to the front of her white apron and crossed above the waist. At her single nod, the straps of her white *kapp* dangled, and Sawyer led the way up the wooden steps. Anna turned a smug look on her brother and said, "It seems we have three guests tonight, *brudder*. I hope you don't mind I invited Fannie Beiler for dinner tonight. She's such a nice girl." Anna waved Naomi into her home first. As Naomi crossed the threshold, Anna said, "She's dependable. Fannie would never turn her back on her loved ones. That would be so cruel, isn't that right, Naomi?"

At the meaning behind Anna's words, Naomi stumbled and froze right inside the entry of what should have been a hospitable Amish home.

But Naomi felt no warm welcome from the homeowner, and even questioned the safety of being there.

Sawyer cringed at Anna's sharp tongue. He had been expecting her to be upset, but not vindictive. Once Naomi walked into the home, he held back and said under his breath, "We will talk later, but for now, you are to show charity. Lives are at stake. Can I trust you to do this?"

Anna looked to the baby in his arms, then back at him. She gave a single nod with pursed lips. She wasn't happy about complying, but Sawyer was satisfied to see his sister had some sense. There was more to the story than what she saw. There was even more to the story than what Naomi had shared with him and the police.

That Sawyer was certain sure of. And when the time was right, he would find out the truth.

All of it.

"She'll need a room and a cradle," he said to Anna.

"I'll have Esau get it from the basement."

"Denki."

Anna lifted her chin at him. "Don't forget your Amish ways, *brudder*. There is no need to thank me. Aid to each other is expected."

"Well, for now I need you to consider her one of us and offer her the same aid." At Anna's sigh of agreement, he held the door for his sister, and let her go before him.

A long, plain white hallway void of any adornments extended from the door with a staircase off to the right. The great room with the kitchen opened up at the end of the hall, and Naomi had stopped at the entry to wait for them. The look of concern on her face showed her trepidation about going in. The family, and apparently, a certain dinner guest were on the other side. Sawyer wondered at the additional hurdle he would have to deal with tonight with Fannie seated beside him. It figured his sister would choose today to play matchmaker, and he was certain sure Anna had arranged the seating to her liking.

Anna stopped in front of Naomi, and the two women shared a tepid moment of silence.

Naomi spoke first. "Please let me know how I can help you in return for your hospitality."

"You'll have your hands full with your baby, but if the need arises, I will let you know. For now, run upstairs. In the first room on the right is a dress on the bed. I just laundered it. Put it on." Anna moved past her swiftly and announced to the room they had another guest. Sawyer relaxed a bit hearing Anna put on a cheerful demeanor to her family. They would follow her lead and welcome Naomi's presence without fear.

Naomi walked back down the hall to the staircase.

She paused in front of Sawyer and took Chloe from him. The two would go in together. "I hope neither of us regrets this," she said.

"The other option is putting your life and Chloe's in jeopardy, and I know we would regret that more."

"Ya," she said, the dialect slipping back into her vocabulary seamlessly as though she had never left.

But she had.

Sawyer would do well to remember that fact. He cleared his throat and waved for her to ascend the stairs ahead of him. He followed her up and retrieved an infant's gown from his youngest niece's room. It would be large on the infant, but Chloe would pass as an Amish child regardless.

Sawyer went back downstairs to wait for them to dress. Standing at the bottom of the steps, he fiddled with the round wooden top of the staircase's newel post. It moved in his grip, and he made a mental note to repair the railing system. Being at home more, he would be able to help his sister with repairs. As he made a mental list of items that he would need from his workshop to complete the repair, the wood floor above him creaked.

Sawyer lifted his face and stopped breathing.

For a few moments, the past eight years drifted away with each step Naomi took toward him. She cradled Chloe in one arm, while her other glided down the railing as she descended the stairs. The picture before him had once been an image from his dreams. His Naomi and their child coming to him.

Besides the Amish dress, Naomi had parted her curly blond hair in the traditional Amish style of the community and covered her head as best she could with one of Anna's *kapps*. Her curls still came loose and fell on the sides of her face. Tucking them behind her ears, she then held herself demurely with each step down. When she reached him, she said, "I left our clothes in the bag I brought in Anna's room. I hope that's okay."

Sawyer's mouth had gone dry, and all he could do was nod. It didn't matter that her words were nothing important. They still affected him as if they were a profession of love from her perfect lips. Lips that he yearned to kiss again.

"Is everything all right?" she asked with a quizzical look at him. "You don't look well."

No. Nothing is all right. Nothing is right at all. The defiant thoughts bounced around his head, but Sawyer grasped hold of the Amish way of self-control and reined in his emotions. There was no time or point to resurface nonsensical dreams that would lead nowhere. To spend one moment in them put lives at risk. His thoughts from here on could only be about protecting Naomi and Chloe…so they could safely return to their life elsewhere.

"The whole community has heard about the shooting at the store," he said. "I'm hoping that will keep people from asking about our houseguests for a little while. For now, we'll say you and Chloe are distant cousins visiting. We'll say you are a recent widow in need of a home. That should keep people from gossiping."

"Oh, okay. If you think that's best. What if someone asks about who I was married to? And why my community didn't help me? This could backfire if someone looks into the community I supposedly came from."

"Give just enough to appease them, but you can say

it still hurts too much to share. People will give you time to mourn. Time for you and your baby to heal after a great loss."

Naomi took a deep breath and looked at the happy baby in her arms. She smiled sadly down at the infant with a genuine look of pain on her face. Sawyer wondered if his concocted story wasn't too far from the truth. There had to be a man in Naomi's life, even if they weren't married, as Naomi had told the sheriff.

Had the man died?

Part of Sawyer hoped that was the case, because the idea of Naomi aligning herself with a man who would leave a mother to raise his child alone caused an uncontrollable anger to roil within him. Sawyer would never have done that to her. He would never have put her in such a situation to begin with.

His fists ached, and he realized he had them clenched so tight his nails cut into his palms. Releasing them, he said, "I will do everything in my power to keep you both safe. Do you believe me?"

She lifted an astonished gaze to him. With a slow nod, an appreciative smile swept over her face and her eyes glistened. "Thank you, Sawyer. You have no idea how your words have comforted me. Yes, I believe you."

She took his breath away again with such adoration on her face.

It's for the baby. He chided himself to remember Naomi had left him for the fancy English world. He hadn't been enough to keep her, and that hadn't changed. But he would still protect her, with his life, if need be. He cleared his throat and said, "Shall we go in? They're waiting for us to begin."

"I'm ready to get this show on the road." With no timidity, she stepped in front of him to lead the way. He wondered when she had become so strong. She had faced a gunman today, and now walked boldly into another possible lion's den. Whatever she'd faced in the eight years since he'd seen her had toughened her.

Gut. She would need every ounce of strength to survive the danger ahead.

FIVE

Naomi dried the last dish, stacking it on the open shelf with the rest of the dinnerware. After placing the towel on the wooden peg to dry, she untied her borrowed apron and hung that beside it. The sight of her dark purple Amish dress beneath it brought on a wave of nostalgia. She felt like she was playing dress up, but this was real life to the Amish. There was nothing pretend about them and their lifestyle. To think otherwise would be ignorant of her.

She felt a tug on the back of her dress. Turning around, she found the youngest child of Anna and Esau. Little Ben smiled up at her, and she saw he resembled his uncle Sawyer.

Naomi knelt down to meet him at his level. "What can I do for you?" She poked him in the nose.

The child placed his hand beside his mouth in a conspiratorial way and leaned in to whisper, "Are there any cupcakes left?"

"Oh, no you don't," Naomi chided the boy. "You won't get me to sneak you a treat."

"It's not for me. It's for *Onkle* Sawyer. He told me to come ask you for one."

Naomi looked over the boy's head and found Sawyer standing across the long room by the woodstove. He stood with his arms crossed, listening to whatever Fannie was telling him. He nodded periodically, seemingly interested in the young girl's exuberant tale.

Then he glanced Naomi's way and raised his eyebrows at her.

Naomi smirked at him. He was looking for her to bail him out of the conversation. "Ben, tell your *onkle* I think there are two left for him and his friend. But they should take them outside and eat them on the picnic table. The kitchen is all cleaned up."

She stood and opened a cloth napkin and placed the remaining two chocolate cupcakes Anna had made on it. She pulled up the cloth's edges and turned to find the boy back over by Sawyer relaying the message.

Scanning the room, she found Anna and her husband and two daughters playing with Chloe. The baby was cradled in Anna's arms and laughing at the girls' silly antics.

Naomi smiled at the sight. The baby was handling the loss of her mother with a bit more ease here in this peaceful and joy-filled place.

Ben came running up and pulled on her dress again. He whispered, "He said to bring them outside and don't tell anyone."

"All right, it's our secret."

Naomi looked at Sawyer as she made her way to the back door. She held up the napkin to show him and stepped out onto the porch. The picnic table was down the steps and in the yard. A large oak gave it some shade. As she made her way there, she scanned the horizon and landscape. Nothing but pasture and cornfields were before her. The place brought her such peace that she was certain sure the killer would never find her here. Not that she could stay forever. But for now, she had space to relax and regroup.

She placed the cupcakes on the table and turned to return to the house. But the sight of Sawyer stepping down the stairs stopped her.

He was alone.

Naomi looked back at the house. When he stood in front of her, she asked, "Where's your friend?"

"I asked her to tell Anna the story she told me. It's really intriguing."

Naomi pursed her lips. "That is not nice, Sawyer. I think she really likes you."

"Well, now she knows not to." He walked by her and sat down at the table. "Join me. I can't eat both of these."

"Then why did you ask for both?"

"In case you wanted one while we chatted. Now, sit. We have lots to discuss. And while the family has company, we'll be left alone and have some privacy."

Naomi glanced back out at the fields. "I was just thinking how peaceful it is here. I feel safe, even though I know someone out there wants me dead. In this moment and in this place, I can almost forget."

"Well, don't." Sawyer broke off a piece of the cupcake and tossed it in his mouth. He chewed and spoke around the confection. "That could leave you unprepared for the worst." He swallowed before continuing, "We need to discuss the possibility that you will be found. We need to form a plan. Sit." He waved at the empty bench across from him.

Naomi frowned, but took the seat. She huffed in amazement. "I can't believe it was just yesterday that I was living my ordinary life. It feels like at least a week has gone by with all that has happened. I wish I could go back and change everything."

"Back to yesterday? Or further back than that?" he asked in midbite, the cupcake piece frozen inches from his lips while he waited for her to reply.

Naomi stilled. She gave no response. Then she reached for the cupcake, but she didn't mean to eat it. She picked at the top, and a few crumbs formed and fell on the table. When she spoke, it was a whisper. "It doesn't matter. Going back to any date isn't an option. There's no sense dwelling on it." She put the cupcake back on the napkin and brushed the crumbs away in front of her. Staring straight at him, she said, "I've learned these last eight years all we can do is move forward. The past means nothing anymore."

"I see." Sawyer put his own half of a cupcake down and threw the piece in his hand into the grass. "So, fine." He brushed his hands swiftly. "We move forward."

"Sawyer, I didn't mean—"

He held up a hand. "You're right. No need to apologize. We won't be prepared if we're not focused on the danger at hand. What is done is done. We can't change the past. But we can change what is to come if we're prepared for the worst. So in order to protect you, I need to know what the worst is."

"The worst?" The air rushed from Naomi's lungs as she searched his pointed stare for what he was asking.

She didn't think he really wanted to know how horrid things had been for Debby. Or for her either. Naomi always found people never wanted to hear the details of her attack. They couldn't handle them, no matter how much they said they could. "Let's just say the person who killed Debby meant for her to be in pain. He is stronger when his victim is fearful. He is empowered by our weakness."

"Our?" Sawyer said without hesitancy.

Naomi glanced down at her folded hands. She'd said too much. "I just meant first Debby, and now Chloe and me. He came after me too, you know." She lifted her gaze and found such anger in Sawyer's eyes that her breath caught, and her hands clenched together tight. "You're so different," she said cautiously. "Not like I remember you at all. Not like I remember the Amish."

"The Amish, which you left." He blinked and his anger dispersed to mere annoyance. He looked up into the limbs of the oak tree hanging over them. As he sighed, Naomi studied his rigid jawline, realizing for the first time that it was free of a beard. When he married Liza, he would have had to let his beard grow. Its absence was just another aspect of Sawyer's ways that didn't follow the Amish *ordnung* of rules.

"I've only been back here for a day, and I see you haven't stayed true to the ways either."

He leveled a stare at her. "How so?"

Naomi took a deep breath then nodded at his chin. "No beard." She glanced in the direction of the barn. "A laptop." Facing him again, she said, "Just to name a couple things I've noticed."

He lifted his hand to his chin and brushed the

backs of his fingertips across his clean-shaven face. He shrugged once and said, "I started to grow it, but…" He frowned as his voice trailed off. "Well, when Liza got sick so soon after the wedding, shaving was easier… and better for her."

Naomi squinted. "How so?"

"Her cancer made her blind. She… When she wanted to see me, she would hold my face. I thought a beard would get in the way of her simple attempt to remember what I looked like, so I went back to shaving."

Instant tears sprang up in Naomi's eyes. The image Sawyer portrayed of himself and his wife—her best friend—depicted a sweet love and intimacy. Up until this point, Naomi had done her best to deny the two of them could have had something so endearing—something that was supposed to have been hers. But here was the proof she needed so she could see otherwise.

"It was a marriage of love," she said quietly.

Sawyer caught her gaze with sad eyes, but his expression hardened quickly as he inhaled sharply through his nose. With a lift of his strong chin, he said, "Liza loved with her whole heart, if that's what you mean."

"She always did. She used to have this saying. 'What does your mind say? What does your heart say? And—'"

"'What does *Gott* say?'" Sawyer finished for her. "It was her compass in every decision she made. She only wanted to do what aligned with *Gott*'s will for her life."

Naomi reminisced sadly about her old friend. "I wish—"

"Stop," Sawyer cut her off from going down that road any further. "No wishing will change anything."

"I know. I guess somewhere deep inside me I always thought I would see her again."

"So you could tell her goodbye to her face this time and hurt her more?"

Naomi flinched and fisted the deep purple dress in her hands. "That's not fair. I never wanted to hurt her."

"No, that pain was only for me."

Naomi looked to the house to see Anna standing on the back porch. The anger on her face matched her brother's sitting across the table. Once again, coming to this farmstead didn't feel like a good idea.

"Perhaps you can take me over to my parents' home, so I can see about staying with them. I'm sure they would let me stay in their barn at least." Naomi pressed her lips tight, not wanting to face the fact that they would most likely turn her away completely.

"You're staying here, where I can make sure you're safe."

Naomi reached across the table and covered his folded hands in front of him. Her touch jerked him visibly, and she pulled back. "I'm sorry. I didn't mean to cross a line. I know I hurt you, and I will forever be sorry for that too, but if staying here upsets you this much, I don't think I should be here."

"I'm fine," Sawyer said with an attempted look of indifference to her presence. His back straightened, and the smile he forced made her smirk.

Shaking her head, she said, "If you call this fine, then I'm even more concerned about being here."

"Well, I just can't pretend your leaving didn't cause problems here. Liza was crushed. I just think you should know that."

Naomi sighed and glanced at Anna. Her arms were folded at her waist and she wore a scowl. "And your sister?"

Sawyer followed Naomi's gaze and glanced over his shoulder. "What about her?" He turned back to face Naomi. "She witnessed Liza's pain too."

"I see," Naomi said, knowing he really meant his own. "If there had been any other place to take Chloe, I would have gone there instead. Perhaps Sheriff Shaw knows of a place."

Sawyer stood abruptly. "I said you're staying here. Now, that's the end of it. Do you understand?"

Naomi glanced up at the towering man. His annoyance came through with a pointed finger jammed down on the wooden table. "I understand. But I also need to feel safe here, Sawyer." She glanced at Anna again.

"Not a hair on your head will be touched while you are under my protection. I promise you that."

"Why do you care so much? We both know I hurt you more than anyone."

Sawyer's eyelids dropped closed and he turned his face toward the barn. In a sigh, he spoke without looking back at her. "Chloe needs her mother. That's all. As long as I have the capability to make sure not another person is hurt by your leaving, whether on purpose or not, I will be there."

"For Chloe," Naomi said.

He looked at her directly. "For Chloe."

With that he stepped away from the picnic table and made his way toward the barn. As he passed the house, he called up to his sister, "Give my farewell to Fannie, please."

"You should do it yourself," Anna clipped back.

"I didn't invite her. Next time, a warning would be nice. Or better yet, let's not have a next time. It's never going to happen for these girls. Not with me."

"Because you plan to return to *her*?" Anna jutted her head in Naomi's direction.

Sawyer scoffed and glanced back at Naomi. "I can tell you that will never happen either." And with that, he left them all behind.

The wind whipped and rustled through the tree leaves as the women watched Sawyer's retreating back. He reached the barn and closed the doors behind him on a creak.

"Did you hear that?" Anna broke the awkward silence once Sawyer disappeared. She looked smugly down from the porch.

All Naomi could do was nod.

"Good. Because I don't plan on letting you forget it."

Anna's brother had just given his sister the ammunition she needed to put Naomi in her place. Whether Sawyer realized it or not, he had compromised Naomi's safety here. Anna might not touch one hair on Naomi's head, but she had the ability to cut through more than hair, and even skin.

Anna could cut right through to Naomi's heart if she wanted to. And judging by the flaming daggers in her eyes, she wanted to. Perhaps Sawyer was wrong, and there was as much danger here on the farm as there was off it.

SIX

With the moonlight streaming in through the window, Naomi put Chloe down in the borrowed cradle and watched her fall back into a deep slumber. Just beyond the plain white walls Anna and her *mann* also slept. And somewhere in the house, Sawyer roomed, though Naomi wasn't sure where because he never returned to the house after their discussion at the picnic table.

Or, more accurately, after he'd made his disdain for her clear.

It was almost as if he knew all about her secret.

She scoffed. It wasn't possible. She had never told anyone from Rogues Ridge, because she had left town the night of the party. A chill ran up her spine and shook her just thinking about that night down at the closed-down coal mine. The English teenagers had gathered in the vacant manager's home to imbibe in alcohol with no supervision around. Sawyer had warned Naomi and Liza they could get into trouble, but only Liza had heeded his warning and stayed home.

Naomi had never dreamed that trouble would leave her beaten and violated.

Some would say things got out of hand, but for Naomi she often wondered if she'd been singled out because she was Amish.

She looked out her bedroom window but saw another window in her memory. The second-floor gabled window she'd tried to reach when someone had grabbed her from behind and covered her mouth to keep her from screaming for help. She'd fought to be released, but she was thrown down on the wood floor and hit her head hard enough to weaken her ability to fight back and protect her virtue. Sometime in the night, after she'd been broken and cast aside, she'd made her way down the stairway and out to the back of the house. She'd collapsed by the dumpster, feeling like the refuse that the large containers were used for. If it hadn't been for the kind man who'd found her, she didn't know what would have happened to her. He got her cleaned up and made a way for her never to have to tell Sawyer he had been right that night.

No, there was no way Sawyer knew about what happened to her. His disdain for her was totally because he believed she left him because she didn't want to marry him.

He couldn't be more wrong.

But to tell him would mean she would have to tell him about that night, and she couldn't do it.

Naomi would think that after marrying Liza for love, he would have let go of his scorn toward her.

Love.

She tried to imagine Sawyer and Liza in a loving marriage, but it was impossible. Liza was always so shy and quiet. Naomi had known her friend fancied

Sawyer in secret, but he barely knew she was alive. He was too gregarious for someone like Liza. It was like a mouse and lion partnering up. Eventually the lion would swallow the mouse alive.

Was that what happened? Naomi wondered, but quickly shook her head. Their relationship was none of her concern. Her only thoughts needed to be on protecting this innocent child from someone who meant her harm. The only man Naomi needed to focus on was Debby's attacker. The man who left Debby pregnant might have returned to erase any evidence of his assault.

Naomi stepped away from the sleeping baby and walked up to the window. The full moon beamed bright and shone down on the farm and barn nearly as bright as day. She thought of Sawyer's workshop in the rear of the barn. Somewhere in there was his laptop he used for business. She could easily slip out right now to do a little searching, and she wouldn't have to explain to anyone why she was using it. Or tell them who she was looking for.

She knew the name only because Debby said it in her sleep one night right before Chloe was born. Debby had been restless in her last month of pregnancy. She'd feared the father would return and find out she had a baby. Her dreams, or rather nightmares, had become so vivid in her last month, and she called out words.

One time she called out a name.

Naomi hadn't wanted to believe it to be the baby's father. She knew the name. It was unique enough to stand out.

Irv Adams.

There was a Louisville attorney by the name Irving Adams. Could he be the same man who'd raped Debby? The same man who'd fathered Chloe? He would have a lot to lose if the truth came to light. His business, at least. Was there anything else he feared losing? Feared it enough to kill to protect it.

Naomi pressed her lips tight. While the house slept, she could sneak out and see what the internet could offer. A glance back at Chloe affirmed the baby was sound asleep and most likely would be until dawn.

With the decision made, Naomi slipped a shawl over her shoulders and made her way out the bedroom door and down the hall. She took the stairs one silent step at a time. Not one tread creaked beneath her, and she breathed a sigh of relief.

Then she touched the newel at the bottom step and the round top knob twisted and toppled off. Naomi moved fast, but the round top juggled in her hands as she struggled to catch it firmly and stop it from crashing to the floor. In the tussle she fell to her knees, hitting them hard before the wooden top rested securely in her arms and under her chin.

She held her breath to listen for any response from above. She knew she hadn't been very quiet in her fall, even if the wooden top hadn't hit the floor. But when no commotion stirred above, Naomi carefully stood and righted the knob back in its place as gently as possible. Giving it a soft pat, she turned to the hall that led to the back of the house and crept toward the rear exit. Careful not to disturb anything else and bring awareness to her endeavor, she opened the door and stepped out into the cool night. Passing by the picnic table she and Sawyer had shared earlier that evening, she took a quick look and reflected on the strange feeling that lingered from their conversation. Strange because she didn't understand why his marriage of love affected her. She always knew he would marry and love his *fraa* with all he had in him. Sawyer never did anything half-heartedly.

She smiled as she remembered a time when he tried to get her attention from one of the boys who fancied her. Sawyer made a spectacle of himself as he challenged Thomas Beiler to a buggy race. He nearly upended his buggy when Thomas proved to be much faster. But instead of accepting defeat, Sawyer stood up and shouted how he felt about her at the top of his lungs before Thomas crossed the finish line. Poor Thomas never got to enjoy the moment of victory, because Sawyer made sure he would have the real victory first.

He loved her.

And didn't mind the whole community knowing.

When courting was typically kept secret, even from the families, Sawyer shouted his feelings for her to anyone who could hear in a mile radius.

The responses from most of her friends had been smiles of approval. Of course, Thomas hadn't been smiling. She'd expected that, but she never expected Liza to respond the same way. That was when Naomi realized Liza had a secret crush that she kept even from her best friend.

Naomi wasn't surprised Liza would agree to marry Sawyer.

She was surprised he loved her.

She shook the feeling away and returned her focus

on something she could figure out—Debby's attacker's name. If his identity could be confirmed, there just might be a path to the man who killed her, then came to Rogues Ridge for Chloe.

The closed barn doors loomed ahead in the full moonlight. When she reached the barn, she looked back at the house and didn't notice any stirring. There was no light in the house, the windows dark.

Naomi lifted the latch to one door, and it opened with barely a creak. After widening it just enough to slip inside, she closed it behind her but left it unlatched.

In the darkness, she felt her way with a faint stream of moonlight to the back workshop. At the door, it opened with ease, and she was glad Sawyer kept it unlocked. He would have no reason to lock it up from family, but Sawyer seemed to do things the Amish didn't typically do.

Naomi located a lantern on the hook by the door and quickly had a fire burning bright. Holding it up, she let the flame guide her toward the table that he used as a makeshift desk. She placed the lantern on the tabletop and opened the drawer beneath it. She breathed a sigh of relief when she saw the laptop. She bent down and reached in for it, just as a whooshing sound went by above her. In the next second a thudding sound alerted her to something hitting the wall. A vibration followed as she saw the reflection in the firelight on something shiny before her.

A saw blade protruded out from the wall and still vibrated from its impact.

The jagged curves of the blade's edge could have ended up in the back of her head if she hadn't bent down. Naomi stared at the menacing tool meant to cut wood but which had been used to nearly kill her.

Total fright scared all the air from her lungs as she processed how close to death she had come. Her mouth opened to scream, but before a sound emitted from her lips, a strong arm appeared from behind and a hand stifled her plea for help from the people who slept soundly in the house, having no idea the killer had found her.

"She's snooping," Anna said from behind Sawyer in the dark kitchen. "You should not have brought her here. She can't be trusted."

Sawyer sighed because he had no reply to justify why Naomi would be in his workshop. The faint light of a lantern through the barn window showed where she was inside, looking for who knew what.

"There's nothing in there of interest for her. Nothing to snoop," he reasoned aloud, a bit irritated he had to vouch for Naomi to his sister so soon after he brought her here. Naomi couldn't even wait one night before putting him in such a predicament. Sawyer remembered another time she'd left him to make the excuses.

With answers he didn't have.

"I'll go find out what's going on," he said and opened the back door.

"*Gut.* We need to know why she chose Rogues Ridge."

Sawyer looked over his shoulder at Anna. "She chose it for safety."

"Don't be so naive, *brudder.* She could have gone anywhere in the world. She's here for other, more personal reasons."

Sawyer didn't respond. He only shut the door behind him and made fast work in reaching the barn. But just as he reached the double doors standing ajar, a crash resonated from inside, followed by a piercing scream.

Naomi.

Sawyer grasped both doors and yanked them wide at the same time. His first thought was something had fallen on her, but when she screamed again, he heard pure fear in her voice. His feet ran and stumbled a bit in the darkness, not moving as fast as he willed them to.

Another scream brought tears to his eyes when he couldn't reach her fast enough to make whatever was happening to her stop.

"I'm coming, Naomi," he yelled as he reached his workshop door. But a twist of the doorknob didn't work. He shook it in a panic, but quickly stepped back and gave the thin door two hard kicks before it splintered and cracked enough for him to push himself through.

"Naomi!" he yelled in the shadowy room. Lantern light flickered at the back, and he noticed a dark figure head for the back door. Before he could make out who it was, the person lifted the lantern and threw it into the workshop.

Contact with various chemicals instantly ignited flames on a whoosh. Sawyer shrank back, his hands raised to protect his face. Had Naomi started the fire?

He glanced at the rear doorway, left open to the pasture beyond.

The thought of such malice pounded in his head. Had Anna been right? Had Naomi returned for her own personal vendetta? But no, she had been shot at. He'd witnessed it.

Or she'd set the whole scene up.

The idea sickened his stomach.

"Why, Naomi?" he yelled as he ran to the back to save his work and his sister's barn. He grabbed a covering draped over a dining room table that was recently finished. Racing to the growing flames, he threw it over the fire and tamped it down with his boots. "Come back here!" he shouted. "And explain yourself! Do you hate me this much?"

No response came, and the doorway remained empty.

Two more stomps, and the fire was snuffed out enough for him to run to see where she went. But as he ran past where his desk lay turned upside down, something in the wall by his head caught his eye. With no time to figure it out, he ran past it for the door. But at the opening, nothing but a still night lay before him. With the moonlight, he scanned the fields beyond the fence, but with no sight of Naomi, he turned back to survey his smoking workshop. With the moon behind him, he could see things more clearly in the room. And the first thing he noticed was the piece of metal protruding from the wall.

A saw blade had been impaled into the wall.

Had Naomi thrown it?

Or had someone thrown it at her?

"Naomi!" he yelled. Pure terror threaded his voice. He turned in a circle, searching the workshop in a panic. Was she still in here somewhere? Hurt by the person he'd seen throw the lantern? A race around the room came up empty, and he scanned the pasture beyond the door. A sinking feeling overcame him. It reminded him of the last time he realized she was gone. Eight years ago, he had been left to realize he wasn't enough to keep her.

Now he realized he wasn't enough to keep her safe.

SEVEN

Naomi didn't dare stop running or look over her shoulder for even one second. Her bare feet hit the hard dirt path at a rapid rate, and her heartbeat kept up with them. All she could think about was escaping from the man who just tried to kill her…again. She had to thank her self-defense coach for the techniques he had drilled into her and her support group. The training was part of their sessions. It empowered the women to take back their lives and feel safe again. But part of Naomi had always doubted she would remember enough to actually save herself.

Tonight proved otherwise.

The moves came from deep within her muscle memory and quickly took the man by surprise. One moment, she couldn't breathe with his hand over her mouth, and the next, she had him on the ground. It gave her enough time to put distance between them, so she could get away. Maybe if she had known how to break free from a hold eight years ago, she wouldn't have had to run away from Rogues Ridge in the first place. And yet, even after breaking free this time, here she was running again.

It didn't matter that she could be leading this man to an isolated place to finish the job. If it meant she led him away from Chloe, then she would keep running for as long as she needed to.

Or until she ran out of path.

Naomi knew somewhere around here was a stream that flowed into the river. She knew she would reach the banks of that water soon, and depending on the place she came to, it could be impassable or wadable. Either way, it was going to slow her down and she could be caught.

Unless she wasn't being chased at all, because the man didn't come for her, but Chloe.

Naomi's feet stumbled at the thought. Had she just left the baby unprotected and alone? The man would know she wasn't with the baby. He would now have access to her with no one to stop him.

The whole house was asleep. He could slip in with no one noticing.

Instant concern had Naomi slowing her steps and turning an ear to any sounds behind her. No other footsteps but hers made a sound. He must have stayed behind. He could already be in the house.

Naomi prayed for God to wake Sawyer up. She'd never make it back in time. Even so, Naomi had to try. She had to get to the baby and protect her with every breath she had in her. She had to protect her with her life.

Naomi picked up her steps and rushed back to the farm. The moon lit her path and kept her from stumbling, but up ahead she could see tree branches hanging over a shadowed portion. She'd run through this path already, but now running toward danger stirred up fear as her feet closed in on the darkness. Naomi envisioned Chloe, alone in the bedroom, and pressed on at full force. She picked up her speed with determination to reach the child before this killer. With the child's safety at the forefront of her mind, a tunnel vision formed before her with only Chloe's face to lead the way.

Naomi ran forward blindly. Strength and power grew in every footfall. It was as though her muscles multiplied instantly and her feet carried her farther and faster than ever before in her life. Something in her switched over, and nothing would stop her from protecting her child.

But no, not her child. Debby's baby.

Her mind attempted to straighten that fact out, even though all internal intuition said otherwise. All that mattered was that there was a child in danger.

Darkness descended as she entered the tree covering. Now she ran blindly, her feet falling in unknown places. She raised her hands before her for protection if she fell. Her feet stumbled over rocks and tree roots. Then she smacked straight into a tree.

No, not a tree.

Her hands fumbled frantically as her mind registered that a formidable man stood before her. Her mouth opened and a scream struggled out.

"Naomi!"

Her name was yelled, but the voice was muffled in her ears. Then strong hands gripped her upper arms and squeezed.

Words were shouted in her face, and she realized it was Sawyer before her. It had been him she had plowed into. It was Sawyer who held her firmly now, trying to calm her screams.

He pressed her close into his chest as her fingers grasped hold of his cotton nightshirt. "What happened?" he demanded.

As Naomi realized she was safe with Sawyer, she also registered the fact that Chloe was left even more vulnerable without Sawyer's protection back at the house.

"Chloe!" she cried and pulled away. "I have to get to Chloe before he does."

Naomi took off in a run again, but this time she had Sawyer beating a path beside her. "Who is he?" he shouted. "I want the truth from you."

"You don't want the truth," she said through pants of breath. "The truth comes with responsibility, and it means walking alone."

"You're wrong. I want to help you! Why did you leave the safety of the house? Were you looking for this man? Were you looking for Chloe's father? The man who left you to raise his child alone. Tell me! Were you looking for Chloe's father?"

"I was, but it's not what you think," Naomi cried as the silhouette of the house came into view. Gaslights, blurred through her tears, shone from the baby's room and propelled Naomi's feet faster.

Then she was halted to a stop. Sawyer had grabbed her arm and pulled her back, jarring her teeth. "The truth, Naomi!" He angrily loomed above her, demanding what she could never give him.

Stunned, she searched his stern face. Moments ticked by. Critical moments. Her gaze shot beyond his shoulder at the dark shadows of the farm behind him. In any of the hidden places, the man could be lying in wait to take a shot at them.

Or he could already be in the house.

She yanked her arm from his grasp and stepped away. "If you can't help me without knowing the truth, then I will do this alone."

She turned her back and took off in a run, doing just that.

The cool of the night brushed over Sawyer as he stood in the middle of his sister's farm and stared up at her home.

Not his.

Never his.

No matter if he lived out his days here, this place would always be hers and her family's. He would do his part in the everyday workings of the home and farm.

But it would never be his.

As Sawyer watched Naomi race ahead in a determined step, he stood at an impasse. Whether she realized it or not, he too was alone. A forever guest in Anna's home with no change on the horizon. As much as his sister tried to play matchmaker, she would never find him a match. There was nothing wrong with all the girls. *He* was the problem.

Naomi reached the house and took the first porch step. She dived to the top of the porch and scuttled toward the door. He got his feet to engage and moved fast to reach her, needing to stand in the way of any more danger aimed for her. As he ran blindly, the image of the saw blade protruding from his workshop walls flashed in his mind. Naomi hadn't thrown that. Whoever was after her thought he could do it silently without waking the house.

Lights flickered on as his sister's family awoke to Naomi's burst through the door.

Sawyer ran blindly toward a threat he knew nothing about. All he knew was Naomi was involved in something deadly, and whether she trusted him enough to share or not, he couldn't stand by and let her be killed.

His feet pounded on the hard dirt. His breath shortened and labored as he pushed on faster, and when his boots hit the first step of the porch, he made the decision to stand by her even if she kept him in the dark. Naomi and Chloe were in trouble, and that was all that mattered.

He flung open the screen and rushed inside. He immediately heard Anna's angered tone from the back of the house. He looked up at Esau, who stood at the top of the stairs and shouted, "Barricade the doors!"

The two men worked to secure the front of the house, and when Sawyer entered the kitchen, he stopped short.

Naomi faced Anna, who held Chloe away from her.

"Please, give her to me," Naomi begged.

"Not until you come clean of what is going on. What kind of life have you been living that you would put yourself and this child in harm's way? That you would put us in danger!"

"I have told you all I know. Believe me, I have."

"Then what were you doing out in the barn? Who were you meeting?"

"No one," Naomi stated forcefully and lifted her chin. "Now, give me the baby."

Sawyer squinted at her choice of words. *The baby. Not* my *baby.*

Something about the words felt off. He shook the thought away for now.

"Anna, give her the child. Right now we need to make sure the house is secured and safe. Someone is out there with a gun and means harm. We don't need to know the details to help Naomi and Chloe."

Naomi turned her face toward him with a questioning gaze in the lantern light. "Do you mean that?"

"I saw the blade in the wall. And I just heard the gun shoot at you. I don't care why. I just want you safe."

Anna held Chloe firmly. "Well, this is my home, and I do care who we are housing."

"Give Naomi her child," Sawyer instructed his sister again.

"I want to know why she was sneaking around here late at night when we are all supposed to be asleep. If not to meet someone, then why?" Anna looked to him. "I have every right to an answer."

"Give Chloe to her mother."

Suddenly, Naomi began to cry. "You can't give her to her mother." She backed away from Anna and Chloe and dropped her arms to cover her face as she sobbed.

Sawyer took a step closer but stopped short of reaching for her. "What is it, Naomi?"

Naomi sniffed as she visibly pulled herself under control. She dropped her hands and wrapped her arms around her midriff. Lifting her tearstained face to him, she whispered, "You can't give Chloe to her mother."

Sawyer glanced Anna's way. His sister wore the same confused look he figured he did. Anna shrugged at him, and he looked back at Naomi for further explanation. "We don't understand."

Naomi swallowed hard. She sniffed deep and blurted out, "She's dead. Chloe's mother is dead."

With that she turned and walked to the back door. Moonlight streamed in on her through the large window beside the door. The room stilled in a heavy silence.

Sawyer opened his mouth to demand more answers but closed it when he didn't even know where to start. His mind ran through all the scenes that had transpired since the moment Naomi stepped back into his life. He opened his mouth again to ask who Chloe's mother was, but all that came out was, "You lied to me."

Naomi shook her head and faced him. "No. I never said Chloe was my child. You assumed it and—"

"You let me assume it," Sawyer cut her off, hearing the anger in his voice. "That is a lie by omission."

"I didn't know who I could trust. I promised Debby I would keep her baby safe."

"Debby is Chloe's mother," Sawyer said as he put the puzzle together. "Debby is dead."

"I promised her I would protect Chloe."

"From whom?"

"I don't know. That's what I'm trying to figure out. That's why I went into the barn."

Sawyer glanced out through the window. "Outside you told me you were looking for Chloe's father. You thought he was out in the barn?"

Naomi looked to Anna and dropped her gaze. "I wanted to use your laptop to do some searching. I knew

it wouldn't be allowed, so that's why I sneaked out."
She lifted an imploring gaze to Sawyer. "You have to
understand. If I can figure out who he is, I may find
Debby's killer." She took a step toward him, saying,
"Please underst—"

At that moment, the window behind Naomi blasted
in, spraying glass shards inward and sending Naomi
facedown to the floor at his feet. Sawyer dropped immediately beside her.

"Get down!" he yelled to his sister, but Anna had already turned and run with the baby back toward the hall
and out of the line of fire. Esau could be heard pounding down the stairs from where he had stood guard
above. Sawyer could hear his sister and brother-in-law
hollering out, but no words computed in his mind. All
Sawyer could focus on was the woman lying facedown
beside him and not moving.

Blood seeped through the back of her white night-
gown. Shards of glass penetrated her skin, and the
bright red blotches grew with each second.

"Naomi," Sawyer called to her as he bent close to her
head and carefully felt for a pulse against the soft skin
of her neck. His fingers brushed over the strong beat,
and he breathed a prayer of thanksgiving to God. "Stay
with me, Naomi," he pleaded, remembering they were
the same words he said to her when she'd left to go to
an English party eight years ago. The night she chose
the English way of life over him. "Please, stay with me,"
he begged just as he had the night of the party. The last
time he saw her before she left town.

But he couldn't hold her then. Could he now?

Sawyer brushed her loose curls behind her ear to get

a better view of her face. She moaned, slow at first as she came out of unconsciousness. A pained whimper followed, and her body jerked.

"Shh…don't move," he instructed.

"Sawyer," she cried and tried to lift her head. "It hurts. Oh, Sawyer, help me."

"I'm right here. Where does it hurt?"

"My side." She moved one hand to reach for her right side. She winced and inhaled sharply. Her hand came away bloody, stirring Sawyer into action.

"I need to put you on your side. I don't want to turn you on your back because of all the glass. Can I move you?"

Naomi nodded and lifted her hand to him to help. It took only one moment to see the front of her gown was soaked.

"Anna!" Sawyer shouted. "She's been hit. We need to stop the bleeding." He bent close to Naomi again. "I'm so sorry. We're going to help you."

"Chloe." Naomi squeezed his hand and implored him. "Promise me you will keep her safe. I have to know she will be all right."

"You'll know because you'll be here to see for yourself. Just stay with me, and I'll take care of you. I'll take care of you both."

Esau crawled up to Sawyer's side. "I'll help you get her to the hallway. Anna can inspect her safely there. Then we'll check the outside for the shooter."

"No!" Naomi cried out. "Don't go out there." She reached for his face, pressing her palm against his cheek and pulling him close. The fear in her eyes so close to his made him want to promise her anything. But they couldn't sit inside wondering when this man would strike again, waiting for him to. Still, they needed to check her wound and stop the bleeding.

"I'm not leaving your side," he promised her. Not until he knew she was safe. He breathed deeply when she relaxed enough for Esau to take her and drag her to the hallway.

Anna shouted, "Bring me clean cloths, if you can get to the drawer. Otherwise, I'll need your nightshirts."

Sawyer crawled alongside Naomi holding her hand as Esau moved her carefully to the center of the house. As he passed by the kitchen drawers, he let go of her to quickly reach up and take everything in the towel bin. He also ripped his shirt off himself. When he returned to Naomi's side, she lay on her side in the hallway in front of his sister.

Now at his sister's mercy.

"Please, Anna," Sawyer passed the cloths over to her. He locked his gaze on Anna's stern expression. "I can't…"

Lose her.

The unspoken words hung between them. They made no sense when he'd already lost her eight years ago.

Anna's eyes narrowed more. "I'll do my best, but I've only delivered babies. Never bullets."

"Chloe?" Naomi called out.

"I have the child," Esau said. He had taken the baby from his *fraa*. Chloe was wide-awake, taking in the strange scene. Thankfully, she didn't cry in fear, but observed and withheld her response.

Naomi reached out her trembling hand. "Sawyer,

take her somewhere safe. Please protect her. Don't l-let him g-get her. He w-will k-kill h-her."

"She's going into shock," Anna said. "I need to work quickly. Esau, I need blankets."

Esau handed the baby to Sawyer and pushed back into the darkness of the house. Sawyer leaned close to Naomi and put his finger to her trembling lips. He fought the urge to comfort her with his own. "It's going to be all right. Anna will take care of you. And I've got Chloe. You don't have to worry. Just—" He swallowed hard. "Just stay alive. For Chloe, *ya*? Stay alive for Chloe."

Sawyer pulled away to allow Anna to tear Naomi's gown and inspect the wound. At his sister's intake of breath, he nearly pushed her out of the way to take over.

"Go, *brudder*. You're no use to me in your distress. She needs a doctor. Bring Chloe upstairs to stay with the *kinner*. Then if you can safely get to the barn, call the sheriff. And pray," Anna commanded over her shoulder. "Esau will help me with Naomi. I will do my best."

Sawyer stared at the back of his sister's head. Before he could temper his words, he said, "But what if your best for Naomi isn't really your best? We all know how you feel about her."

Anna stilled in her ministrations over Naomi. Sawyer expected her to call him to task, but instead she said, "Then pray for me too. *Gott* knows I will need every prayer if I am going to save her."

EIGHT

"How bad is it?" Naomi whispered through clenched teeth. She'd waited for Sawyer to leave the hallway to ask his sister.

Anna huffed. "I'm not a doctor. Perhaps you should have thought about being somewhere near a medical facility instead."

"I thought about the best place to hide."

"Well, ready or not, you've been found." Anna pressed harder, causing Naomi to inhale sharply. "The entry hole has stopped bleeding. The bullet went straight through and came out your side. It's below your rib cage and only penetrated your waist. I don't think it hit any organs. I can stitch you up if you want."

"You know how to do that?"

"I've assisted enough births, *ya*." Anna unrolled a long piece of thread and cut it. "Sometimes they require a little putting back together." She lifted a hot needle from the lantern's flame and threaded it through the eye.

"How long have you been a midwife?"

"For five years on my own, but a lot longer helping my *mamm* before that."

"So I'm safe with you." Naomi's statement didn't receive a response. The next moment, Anna put a wooden rod in Naomi's mouth.

"I don't mean to hurt you, regardless what you think, but bite down. It will help."

Naomi did as she was told, and in the next moment, the pain of the needle stabbing through her skin had her gripping at anything she could find around her. Her eyes squeezed closed, and her breath locked in her chest. Naomi could feel the thread pulling at her skin as it closed up the bullet wound in her back. Somewhere in the deep recesses of her mind she knew this was only the entry wound. And the smaller of the two holes. After standing up against the pain for a few minutes, Naomi's vision blurred. In and out of consciousness, she remembered a time when her family would have surrounded her in her distress.

Now she had no one. She had to depend on a woman who hated her to help her make it out alive. Naomi figured her own family would feel the same way. It was just as well they weren't here.

She reached out a hand and frantically grasped Anna's wrist. "If something happens to me, will you tell my parents I'm so sorry? I never wanted to hurt them. I never wanted to hurt anyone."

Anna stilled for a moment and pursed her lips. The lantern's flame flickered across her stern face showing her displeasure in the conversation. She took a deep sniff and resumed her stiches without a response.

"I know you don't like me, but I beg of you to think

of my parents instead of me. If I can bring them some semblance of peace, it would help them just as much." The needle pierced harder, cutting off any more words from Naomi's lips. All she could do was breathe deeply and steadily to get through the pain.

When Anna finished the sutures, she tackled the exit wound in Naomi's side. "This one is larger, but I will do my best. How are you feeling?"

Naomi had trouble forming words as her mind felt fuzzy and her muscles weakened. To move her lips to speak required a forced concentration. She managed to say, "Tired."

"Judging by these soaked rags, you've lost a lot of blood. As soon as the police are here, they can bring you to the hospital."

"How?" Naomi whispered. "How did…you call?"

"Sawyer left for the barn. The phone is out there."

Naomi's eyes widened, and she moved an arm to sit up.

"Whoa!" Anna pushed her back. "Don't move. You will restart the bleeding. I'm not sure I'll be able to stop it again."

"But he can't…be out…there. It's dangerous."

"*Ya*, I know. But you didn't think he was going to hide in here and let you die, did you? Regardless of what you think, Sawyer cared a great deal for you."

"Of course, I knew that. I can't let him put his life at risk for me. I have to stop him." Naomi moved her arm to push up again, but Anna was a lot stronger at the moment and kept her from budging.

"You trying to stop him would only put him in more

danger. Let him focus on staying alive out there and not on you. It's the least you can do."

The dig hit Naomi hard. As Sawyer made his way toward the barn, dodging the shooter's gun, he had to only think of himself to stay alive. Without her presence vying for his attention, he could be successful. She would be nothing but a hindrance out there. But Anna's words weren't meant just for tonight. Her return to Rogues Ridge had disrupted Sawyer's life and derailed him off his course of success. He'd already had to move his business to the barn. What else had he had to change because of her presence?

"I shouldn't have come back here." She moved to lie back, then jolted at the slicing pain of the glass embedded in her skin. She cried out and twisted away from the pain.

"*Ach!* Don't move. You started the bleeding again. Your choices are always so poor. You have already hurt so many. Don't you die on me. Sawyer would never forgive me." Anna stitched the shredded skin in her side, causing Naomi to cry out in a pain so blinding, she stopped breathing and the lantern's light diminished as her world went dark.

A fear like nothing Sawyer had ever experienced immobilized him to the confines of the front porch. Before him, the shadowy farm loomed quiet and peaceful, but the wounded woman behind the closed door proved there was nothing peaceful about the scene.

Sawyer covered his mouth to stifle a cry that slipped out from deep within him. He would be no help to

Naomi if he lost it now. He needed to call for help, or he could lose her. *So much blood...*

He pressed his fingers to his eyes, but nothing would erase what had happened right in front of him. He didn't think he would ever forget the sight of Naomi being struck by that bullet. Her face as she went down would never leave him. Nor the way her body lay limp in his arms after.

His breath caught and his throat closed. All he wanted to do was turn back around and race to her side. He needed to hold her, to see for himself that she was alive. He needed to be there for her.

I need to get her help.

The task at hand cut in and forced him to put his own needs aside and focus on the truth. Naomi didn't want him by her side. That was reality. Naomi had chosen the English way of life. That was reality. And now she would die by it.

No, that part didn't have to be real. Whether she wanted his help or not, whether she wanted him or not, he would be true to his Amish ways and offer her aid. He would do whatever it took to keep her alive.

Even face a gunman unarmed.

Sawyer scanned the yard before him. Thankfully the moonlight cast a wide beam over the driveway and pasture, but there were still many dark shadows that the gunman could hide in. What Sawyer wanted to know was how the killer had found Naomi so fast. Had he followed them here?

But why wait to attack then? Naomi had spent the whole afternoon and evening outside before nightfall. Very few people knew she was here. Just the people at the furniture store. Had someone from the sheriff's department informed the killer where he could find her? Even if it wasn't done maliciously but accidently. Either way, Sheriff Shaw would need to investigate. If she had someone on her staff who'd put Naomi and the rest of them at risk, she needed to know.

Right after Naomi was safe. And he needed Cassie and her deputies here for that to happen.

Sawyer took a deep breath. Stepping out into the open had to be avoided. Up until this point, the shooter had stayed hidden, no doubt to protect his identity. Sawyer thought about forcing the man out. Perhaps as he made his way away from the house, the shooter would come out to try to take another shot at Naomi.

Or at him.

No, revealing his position wasn't an option. If the shooter wanted to remain hidden, then so did he. Though stepping into full light would get him to the barn faster, Sawyer would instead navigate the dark corners.

A turn to his left showed the edge of the porch in complete darkness, but on the other side of the railing was pine shrubbery. If he missed his mark, he would land in the greenery and give himself away.

Sawyer took off in a fast run, reaching a hand for the railing as it approached. With one hand on the top, he bent his knees, so his feet landed right on the top of the railing. With all his might, he propelled himself off the railing in a full jump and scaled the tops of the shrubbery, just barely clearing it before gravity pulled his body down in full force.

Sawyer hit the ground and folded his body up to roll

a few times and lessen the impact of the hard ground. After three rolls, he saw the darkness was about to come to an end, and any more rolls would expose him to the light.

But no amount of flailing would slow him down, and the next roll took him from the shadows and out onto the moonlit path to the barn. Not a full breath occurred before the first shot went off. Gravel sprayed up at him where the bullet skidded so close to him.

He didn't wait for another to fly.

Jumping to his feet, he had no choice now but to run straight toward the barn in full moonlight. He pushed to his feet and ran at top speed.

Another gunshot echoed around him, pushing him faster, but it was the sound of sirens off in the distance that had Sawyer praying they were coming his way.

The sound of a car engine roared to life as he closed in on the barn. The sound growing louder, he realized the car was headed straight for him. Dodging a small bullet would prove easier than the front end of a vehicle aimed at him.

Headlights flicked on, drowning him in their high beams and blinding him to the point of pain. Sawyer shielded his eyes but kept running, even as he heard the roar of the car coming straight at him.

Suddenly, the car was on him, and he took a leap up into the air, diving forward in the hope he would escape from being hit. This time there was no time to tuck and roll, and the ground came hard and fast.

But not as hard of an impact as the car would have made. Sawyer had no time to assess any injuries. He crawled away but glanced back just in time to make out a few of the license plate numbers.

B-3-8-3-1 and maybe a *2* at the end. The farther the car raced away down the driveway the darker the plate got, and all that he could see were the red taillights disappearing into the night.

Sawyer jumped up to run the rest of the way to the barn, his only task to get Naomi help. He flung the doors wide and ran toward his office. At the back was the laptop bag and inside was a cell phone for business. He swung the bag down to land on a workbench, tearing into it for the phone.

Frustrating moments ticked by as it powered on and finally the number pad appeared. Pressing 911 hooked him up to an emergency operator, and Sawyer found himself yelling into the phone.

"Sir, calm down and slow down," the dispatcher told him. "I already have a car heading your way. A neighbor heard the shooting. Now, did you say someone has been shot?"

"Yes!" Sawyer took a deep breath and slowed down. "Please send an ambulance. I'm Amish. I can't drive her to the hospital."

Sawyer zipped up the laptop bag and brought it and the phone out of the barn. With the authorities on the phone and on the way, he carefully made his way back to the house. Off in the distance, he could still hear the sirens racing toward him. Red and blue lights swirled at the end of the driveway. A cruiser, but not an ambulance yet.

"Please, *Gott*, help them get here in time," he prayed on the way to the back porch. He climbed the steps and approached the blown-in window Naomi had been standing in front of. Shattered glass spread out in all directions and crunched under his shoes. He opened the door beside the window and entered the house. Once inside, he removed the laptop from the bag to place it on the kitchen table.

"You can't have that in here," Anna said, stepping into the large room and wiping blood from her hands.

Naomi's blood.

Sawyer stared at his sister's hands and swallowed hard the guilt at seeing what Naomi had lost. "How is she?" He ignored Anna's command about the laptop and headed toward the hall, not sure of what he expected to find. He had left Naomi there on the floor, fighting for her life. "Is she—"

"Dead?" Anna finished. "Not yet. But I've done all I can. She needs a doctor. I heard more gunshots. Are you hurt?"

"No. The police are here, and the ambulance is on the way. Where is Naomi?"

"Thank *Gott*," she mumbled and scrubbed at her hand with her blood-soaked apron. "She's still in the hall. Esau is standing guard over her, but she's in and out of consciousness."

Sawyer headed toward the front of the house, but Anna stepped in front of him, putting a hand on his chest.

"You shouldn't go back there. It's not right."

"I need to see her."

"Why? She's nothing to you. You said so. Let the paramedics take her out of here. Let someone else help her from now on. Please."

Sawyer paused to think about what Anna was asking of him. "You want me to turn her away?"

"I want you to let her go. Can you do that?"

Sawyer glanced at the doorway to the hall, then down at the laptop in his hand. He had been ready to search the internet for information on the license plate and car's owner. To let Naomi go would mean letting the search go too.

"Well, can you?" Anna asked again.

Sawyer sighed and closed the cover to return the device back to its bag. "I've let her go before. I should be able to do it again."

"Good. Finally, some reason from you."

Sawyer turned to leave the house.

"Where are you going?"

"To wait for the ambulance and see if I can figure out who was here tonight. They tried to run me over out there, but I think I got the license plate."

"You did?" Anna's voice squeaked.

"*Ya*, why?" Sawyer turned back to look at his sister. "Why does that surprise you?"

Anna shrugged. "It doesn't, but I just asked you to let it go."

"You asked me to let Naomi go. You didn't say anything about letting a killer go. As long as I have breath in me, I have to do what I can to protect my community, and that includes our visitors."

NINE

The rest of the night passed in a blur for Naomi as everyone walked in and out of her room at the Rogues Ridge Hospital. Some were pleased, others were not. The doctor planned to send her home today, even though he didn't understand she didn't have a home to return to. Going back to Anna's house didn't seem like an option. Naomi doubted Anna would allow her to bring more danger into her home. Naomi didn't want to either.

But where could she go now?

Naomi thought of her parents nearby, but she disregarded the idea in an instant. To knock on their door would take more strength than she had in her.

The door to her room cracked open and Sheriff Shaw peeked in. "May I come in?"

Naomi nodded and dropped her head back on her pillow. It felt good to be able to lie on her back now. All the glass shards had been removed, and the cuts medicated. Her side wound would leave a scar, but no internal damage had been done.

"I'm supposed to leave soon," Naomi told Sheriff Cassie when she stepped up to the side of the bed.

"I heard." She frowned.

"You don't like the idea either," Naomi surmised.

"I just got the ballistics report back from the lab. We're dealing with two different shooters. Or at least two different guns. The bullet that hit you came from a rifle. Something a hunter would use. The gunshots at Sawyer's store were from a semiautomatic handgun."

"Maybe they didn't want to miss this time." Naomi swallowed at her own sarcastic remark. "Sorry. I can only say such things because the shooter didn't get me."

Cassie huffed. "The pain in your side when the pain-killers wear off will say otherwise."

"Even so, I'm not down yet."

"That's what I wanted to talk to you about." She touched the side of the bed. "May I sit here?"

Naomi nodded. The seriousness in the sheriff's face created an uneasiness in the room. "Is something else wrong?"

"You tell me."

"I don't understand."

Sheriff Cassie pressed her lips. "Naomi, I can only help you if you are being completely honest and up-front with me. I need to know if there is someone out there who has come after you before, or someone you had an altercation with. Someone who has hurt you in the past. When we talked at the furniture store, I got the impression you had experienced an assault."

Naomi's breathing picked up, and her mind whirred with where this conversation was headed. She shrugged a shoulder in an attempt to end it there, as if it was no big deal.

"Your attack happened here in Rogues Ridge, didn't it?" Sheriff Cassie asked.

"Why does it matter?" Naomi shot a glance in the direction of the door. Cassie had closed it behind her. But that didn't mean someone wasn't on the other side listening. "Do we really have to talk about that? It has nothing to do with this. That was eight years ago. I don't see how rehashing that…that *incident* will help us now."

"Did you not hear me? I said someone is *hunting* you. They nearly succeeded in killing you. Perhaps the person who attacked you before is after you again."

Naomi shook her head in denial. "It can't be someone from here. Debby was killed in Louisville. Her killer came after me here. Hours away."

"Or the killer went looking for you in Louisville and Debby got in the way."

"No. Debby said her attacker had come back and was stalking her. She asked me to take Chloe some-where safe."

"Then why aren't you safe here?" Cassie's eyes stared brightly at her, as if daring her to come clean about that night eight years ago. "You can trust me to keep quiet about whatever you confide in me. I just need the whole story to make sure no surprises pop up. Help me do my job."

Naomi bit her lower lip, not sure where to begin or if she should.

"You mentioned you help women who have been attacked," Cassie said. "If one of them was in danger, and they could protect themselves by being open, what would you tell them to do?"

"To tell, of course. *If* it was safe."

"Well, it is. You can trust me."

Naomi studied the sheriff's serious expression. She seemed authentic and honest, but she also seemed to understand…and care.

Sharing the details of the night of the assault needed to be done.

When Naomi still struggled to know where to begin, Cassie didn't rush her. She didn't speak one word as Naomi formed hers.

"I…I went to a party. An English party. Alone." Naomi folded her hands in front of her, outside the blanket that covered her. "My friend Liza was supposed to go with me, but at the last moment she backed out. Sawyer…" Naomi glanced toward the door and cleared her throat. "He warned me. He said someone would take advantage of me. Of an innocent Amish girl." She looked at her clutched hands, her knuckles white. "I didn't know what he meant. Until it was too late."

At her lengthening pause, Cassie leaned in and covered her hands. "I'm sorry, Naomi. I'm sorry that happened to you. Do you know who it was? Who attacked you?"

Naomi hesitated with a sigh. "I knew you would ask that. Believe me I really don't. I never associated with the English before that night. I didn't know anyone's name, but…" She swallowed hard as her mouth went dry.

Sheriff Cassie's eyebrows rose as she waited for the

One Minute" Survey

You get up to **FOUR books** <u>and</u> Mystery Gifts...

Romance

A Hopeful Harvest
RUTH LOGAN HERNE

You can't always pick who you fall for...

ER PRINT

LOVE INSPIRED SUSPENSE
INSPIRATIONAL ROMANCE

Trained To Defend
CHRISTY BARRITT

UNTAIN GUARDIANS

LARGER PRINT

Suspense

YOU pick your books – WE pay for everything!

See inside for details.

YOU pick your books –
WE pay for everything.
You get up to FOUR new books and TWO Mystery Gift
absolutely FREE!
Total retail value: Over $20!

Dear Reader,

Your opinions are important to us. So if you'll participate in our fa
and free "One Minute" Survey, YOU can pick up to four wonderf
books that WE pay for!

As a leading publisher of women's fiction, we'd love to hear from
you. That's why we promise to reward you for completing our
survey.

IMPORTANT: Please complete the survey and return it. We'll ser
your Free Books and Free Mystery Gifts right away. And we pay
for shipping and handling too! ← *We pay for*
EVERYTHING!

Try **Love Inspired® Romance Larger-Print** books and fall in love
with inspirational romances that take you on an uplifting journey
faith, forgiveness and hope.

Try **Love Inspired® Suspense Larger-Print** books where courage
and optimism unite in stories of faith and love in the face of dang

Or TRY BOTH!

Thank you again for participating in our "One Minute"
Survey. It really takes just a minute (or less) to complete the
survey… and your free books and gifts will be well worth it!

Sincerely,

Pam Powers

Pam Powers
for Reader Service

"One Minute" Survey

GET YOUR FREE BOOKS AND FREE GIFTS!

✓ Complete this Survey ✓ Return this survey

◄ DETACH AND MAIL CARD TODAY! ►

1 Do you try to find time to read every day?
☐ YES ☐ NO

2 Do you prefer books which reflect Christian values?
☐ YES ☐ NO

3 Do you enjoy having books delivered to your home?
☐ YES ☐ NO

4 Do you find a Larger Print size easier on your eyes?
☐ YES ☐ NO

YES! I have completed the above "One Minute" Survey. Please send me my Free Books and Free Mystery Gifts (worth over $20 retail). I understand that I am under no obligation to buy anything, as explained on the back of this card.

☐ I prefer Love Inspired® Romance Larger Print 122/322 IDL GNTG
☐ I prefer Love Inspired® Suspense Larger Print 107/307 IDL GNTG
☐ I prefer BOTH 122/322 & 107/307 IDL GNTS

FIRST NAME   LAST NAME

ADDRESS

APT.#   CITY

STATE/PROV.   ZIP/POSTAL CODE

Offer limited to one per household and not applicable to series that subscriber is currently receiving.
Your Privacy—The Reader Service is committed to protecting your privacy. Our Privacy Policy is available online at www.ReaderService.com or upon request from the Reader Service. We make a portion of our mailing list available to reputable third parties that offer products we believe may interest you. If you prefer that we not exchange your name with third parties, or if you wish to clarify or modify your communication preferences, please visit us at www.ReaderService.com/consumerschoice or write to us at Reader Service Preference Service, P.O. Box 9062, Buffalo, NY 14240-9062. Include your complete name and address.   LI/SLI-520-OM20

© 2019 HARLEQUIN ENTERPRISES ULC
™ and ® are trademarks owned by Harlequin Enterprises ULC. Printed in the U.S.A.

READER SERVICE—Here's how it works:

Accepting your 2 free books and 2 free gifts (gifts valued at approximately $10.00 retail) places you under no obligation to buy anything. You may keep the books and gifts and return the shipping statement marked "cancel." If you do not cancel, approximately one month later we'll send you 6 more books from each series you have chosen, and bill you at our low, subscribers-only discount price. Love Inspired® Romance Larger-Print books and Love Inspired® Suspense Larger-Print books consist of 6 books each month and cost just $5.99 each in the U.S. or $6.24 each in Canada. That is a savings of at least 17% off the cover price. It's quite a bargain! Shipping and handling is just 50¢ per book in the U.S. and $1.25 per book in Canada*. You may return any shipment at our expense and cancel at any time — or you may continue to receive monthly shipments at our low, subscribers-only discount price plus shipping and handling. *Terms and prices subject to change without notice. Prices do not include sales taxes which will be charged (if applicable) based on your state or country of residence. Canadian residents will be charged applicable taxes. Offer not valid in Quebec. Books received may not be as shown. All orders subject to approval. Credit or debit balances in a customer's account(s) may be offset by any other outstanding balance owed by or to the customer. Please allow 3 to 4 weeks for delivery. Offer available while quantities last.

information Naomi withheld. She squeezed her hand and said, "It's okay. You can tell me."

"I just don't know if I remember details correctly. If I knew for sure, I would tell you. Does it really matter anymore?"

"As long as your attacker is still out there, it matters. If you can remember anything about him, please let me know."

"Right now, the only name on my mind is Irv Adams. Debby knew someone by that name. Could he have been her attacker?" Naomi looked to the wall as if the name would be scrawled across its white paint in bright red letters. "It's why I went out in the barn. I was hoping to use Sawyer's laptop, which he has for his English employee, who handles the website. I thought maybe if I did some searching for possible people, I could find a connection to Debby."

"That's my job. I need you to only worry about staying safe and keeping hidden."

Naomi sighed at her predicament. "Do you have another place I can go to hide? I can't return to Anna's house."

Cassie pressed her lips tight. She eyed the door and said, "That's what I wanted to talk to you about. I need to ask Sawyer and Anna how we could stage this, but first, I want to run it by you. I'd like to have them report your death to the community."

Naomi tilted her head. "But I didn't die."

"No one knows that yet. Not even Anna or Sawyer. They are not your next of kin, and I made sure the hospital personnel reported your status to me only. Until I know who alerted that shooter last night, I am trusting no one. For all I know, it was Sawyer who made the call."

"No." Naomi wouldn't believe such a thing. "He—he—"

"He once loved you, and you embarrassed him. He could want retaliation."

"I embarrassed him?" Naomi never thought her leaving would affect him in that way. No one knew he had asked her to marry him. She'd never even told him yes yet. It was their secret. "How?"

At Cassie's cautious face and hesitation, Naomi knew there was more to her remark than she was saying.

"How did I embarrass him? Tell me." She tried to sit up straighter but could only lean forward. "Please."

Cassie looked to the door quickly, then looked back. "I don't know all the particulars, but I grew up in this town too. I remember what people had said right after you left town. I'm not Amish, so I only heard what the English kids were saying about the Amish girl who showed up at the party down by the old coal mine. What they said about you…" She shook her head. "I can only imagine those rumors reached the Amish community too. Teenagers aren't always kind. Either way, your community felt you rejected them and their simple ways. That you chose the English lifestyle and all its negative aspects along with it. That you rebelled fully against them. I'm sure that includes Sawyer. Especially Sawyer."

A heavy silence weighed over them as Cassie's words grew louder in Naomi's head. It couldn't mean what she made it sound like. But what else could she mean?

"All this time…" Naomi whispered. "I thought I was running away to shield them from the truth." She looked up at Cassie's sad eyes. "All this time they believed the worst of me. What am I supposed to do? To go out there and change what they think would mean I would have to tell every one of them the truth. I can't do that."

"Nor should you." Cassie squeezed her hand.

"So I just let them go on thinking the worst of me?"

"Sometimes we have to be okay with being the only one who knows the truth. You don't owe anyone anything, and you could spend your whole life trying to change someone's idea of you before you realized the only people who matter are the ones who believed in you from the start."

"But who are they?" Naomi's voice cracked.

"That's what we need to figure out. Or at least it's my job to figure out who means you harm. If last night's shooter is someone from Rogues Ridge, then that would mean Debby's killer still doesn't know where you are. But it could mean you now have two people hunting you. One who uses a .45 Smith & Wesson and one who uses a .30 aught 6 Ruger hunting rifle. Which I know some Amish homes have for hunting. Not that I'm saying the shooter was Amish. I just have to consider everyone a suspect right now. Even people from your old community."

Naomi thought of her own *daed*'s hunting rifle. Some Amish did have guns. It was possible that the shooter was Amish, even though she couldn't accept the idea of one of them taking aim at a human being. "And you think letting the community think I died would work?"

"If you're dead, no one will come back to try to kill you again. It could buy me some time while the Louisville PD investigates Debby's killer's identity. In the meantime, if someone does return looking for you, then we'll know if someone at Sawyer's house was behind the attack last night. They will be the only people who will know that you're really alive."

"Anna," Naomi said reflectively.

Cassie eyed her. "Would Anna have any reason to want you dead?"

Naomi shifted on the bed uneasily.

"I need to know if you think you're not safe with Anna. I won't send you back there if Anna has any ill will toward you."

"She thinks I'm there to take Sawyer away. She's on a matchmaking endeavor for him and believes I'm in the way. But she saved my life last night."

Cassie gave one last squeeze to Naomi's hand and stood up to leave. "I'll take that into consideration as I look into her motives. I'm sure you're right, and it's just a bit of harmless protectiveness for her brother. Let me worry about Anna, while you worry about getting your strength back. You're going to need every ounce of it if this plan to make it look like you didn't survive the shooting is going to work."

After searching up and down the hallway, Sawyer stood in the middle of the hospital's emergency room. Naomi was nowhere in sight. The last time he saw her was when the paramedics lifted her into the ambulance and whisked her away from Anna's house. Now he couldn't get one word about her status from anyone at the hospital. Had she even been brought here?

"May I help you?"

Sawyer turned to see a woman nurse stepping out from behind a curtain. The patient in the bed was an older man and seemed sedated. "I'm looking for Naomi Kemp. She may have been brought in during the night for a gunshot wound."

The nurse, whose name on her badge read Lynda, glanced down the hall. "I'm sorry, I can't help you." She moved to leave.

Sawyer rushed to step toward her. He raised a hand to hold her off. "Please. Just tell me if she's all right. I don't need to know the details. Did she—"

Die?

The horrible word lodged in his throat. His stomach rolled, and he forced himself to think positively. Naomi had to be somewhere in this place. And she had to be alive. "Please, anything you can tell me…"

"I'll take it from here." He turned at the sound of another woman's deep voice from down the hall. A quick glance showed Sheriff Shaw coming his way.

"Sawyer, come with me. We'll talk in private." The nurse hurried off in relief and left them alone.

Finally, he was going to get some answers. He fell in line behind Cassie, and in a few extra steps he was walking beside her quickly.

"Is she all right?" he asked.

No answer. Just the sounds of their shoes hitting the tile floor and his tight breathing as he was forced to wait longer for the answer to the question he'd been asking for hours. How much longer would he have to wait? What had been only one night had felt like years. But then perhaps this was a question he'd been wondering about for over eight years.

Was Naomi all right? Was she even alive?

He had told his sister he had been able to forget her, that he had let her go. But that wasn't the truth. Not a day went by in the past eight years that Sawyer hadn't asked those two questions. That something in his day hadn't triggered the thought, even for a brief moment of wonder.

Her favorite song sung at church. A buggy race he knew she loved to watch, and even take part in, to her parent's displeasure. A tear on his wife's face when she realized she wouldn't get to say goodbye to her closest childhood friend.

"I need to ask you a few questions about last night." Cassie opened the door to a small, empty office and let him enter first. She closed the door behind her and waved for him to take the chair by the wall. But he remained standing.

She stood with folded hands and widened legs. The hair on the back of his neck rose at what this scene looked like.

"Am I a suspect?" he asked.

"No." Her response came swift and sure. "But I need to know if you own a shotgun."

"No."

"I noticed you are building a gun case in your barn. Why would you need that if you don't own guns?"

Sawyer's breath caught. This was not the direction

he thought things would go in. "It's a special order. For a friend."

"Would your bishop take kindly to you building something so against the Amish's peaceful ways?"

The negative answer stayed behind closed lips, and the floor became his focal point. He had known he had gone too far in agreeing to build this piece of furniture. "It was never going to go in the shop."

"So your bishop would never know. Do you typically sneak behind the *ordnung* like this?"

"No, of course not. There are pieces in my shop that are made for the English only. It's been approved as long as I am not using the furniture. Bishop Bontrager understands it's part of serving the English community."

"But not a gun cabinet. That one you knew you couldn't make in the store, correct?"

Sawyer lifted his gaze. "Can you just tell me how Naomi is? I'll answer any question you want, but I need to know if she's alive. Please."

"And I need to know if you are able to keep a secret, even against your community. The gun cabinet tells me you can. Am I right?"

Sawyer gripped the back of an office chair. "I'm not proud of keeping secrets, but I will if it means Naomi is safe. Please just tell me if she is all right. I can't take waiting any longer."

Cassie leaned back, her eyes narrowing up at him. Slowly, a smile curled on the edges of her lips. "I'm so glad to hear you say this. Please, Sawyer, sit down. I have a lot to discuss with you. Things I will need your cooperation with. But first, Naomi is alive and well."

He let out a deep breath he had no idea had been pent up so tight in his chest. He came around to the front of the chair, and when the backs of his knees hit the edge of the chair, he fell back into it. She was alive.

And well.

"Oh, thank You, *Gott*."

"Yes, and with both of your help, I would like to keep her that way. Can I count on you?"

"I'll do whatever you want."

"Even if it means going against your family? Your sister, in particular?"

Cassie's statement caused concern. "What does Anna have to do with this? She saved Naomi's life last night. If it hadn't been for her, Naomi would have bled out."

"Just as I had to do with you, I have to question if everyone in the home can and will keep this secret. Plus, Naomi tells me Anna is not happy about her return. She could have something to do with the shooting last night."

"But Naomi was being shot at before Anna ever knew she was back in town."

"True, but last night's gunman used a different gun than the first. That means I need to consider multiple shooters. Why would someone with a .45 switch to a basic shotgun for killing varmint?"

"You think someone in the Amish community tried to kill her?"

"I think I need to consider there might be other people who are not happy she is back in town. Someone who thought they got rid of her eight years ago, and now wants to shut her up for good."

Sawyer considered Cassie's ideas for a few moments, but they didn't make sense. "Naomi left because she desired the English lifestyle. No one pushed her to leave."

Cassie frowned. "Maybe. But maybe not."

Sawyer studied her face. "Why do I get the feeling you're not telling me everything?"

Cassie's eyebrows rose. "I don't know. That might be a question for Naomi."

"Except Naomi expects me to let the past go and not ask questions."

"Then honor her wishes and trust that she knows best. And trust me to search under every rock to find this killer."

Sawyer let silence hover for only a few seconds before he nodded his agreement. "What do you need from me to keep Naomi alive?"

Cassie leaned forward, ready to get back to work. "I need you to pretend she's dead."

More silence ensued, but now shock and confusion filled the air. He couldn't have heard her correctly. "Excuse me?"

"You can't tell anyone she's alive. Only your sister and her family, *if* you think Naomi's safe with them. There can be no visitors. Naomi must be hidden. If someone returns to try again, I will have to question the loyalty of your household."

"You can trust them. You can trust all of us," Sawyer said adamantly.

"Even your sister?"

"Anna may have her reasons for not liking Naomi, but she's not a killer. Nor would she ever help one. Esau wouldn't either."

"I hope not. It's Naomi's life I'm charged with protecting. I'm trusting you to help."

"What about the vigil? It's customary to hold the house open for the community to come and pay their respects. Liza's screening took three whole days before the last of the people left."

"There's no need to hold one. Besides, do you really think people would come for a stranger?"

Sawyer frowned and shook his head once, but really out of disgust. "They probably wouldn't come if they knew it was Naomi. But they're wrong about her. They were always wrong about her."

"I'm glad to hear you say that. This won't be easy to pull off. I'll need you to be willing to stand alone."

Naomi's words from last night came crashing back. "She doesn't trust me with the truth."

"Trust is something you earn. If and when Naomi decides to share will be up to her. Can you help her without knowing everything?"

"I'm trying, but there's only so much rejection a person can take. Her distrust in me is a wedge between us that can't be ignored forever."

Cassie stood to leave. She paused at the door and said, "There might come a day when you will wish distrust was the only thing between you."

Sawyer watched Cassie quietly exit the room. She left to make the arrangements for moving Naomi back to the house secretly, but he wondered if he should be the distrustful one, and not Naomi.

He made his way to Naomi's room, slowly at first, but quickly picking up his speed with each step. As her door loomed ahead, he practically ran to it. Knowing she was alive and well on the other side pushed him forward and made him put aside the wedge between them…for now.

Shoving the door wide, he froze at the sight of her sitting up on the edge of the bed. She was ready to go, but by the shock on her face at seeing him, she hadn't expected she would be going with him.

She slowly gained her feet as he said, "I came as soon as Cassie told me where I could find you." He took a step closer to her. Suddenly, a strange awkwardness fell between them. It was nothing either had ever experienced with each other.

Why now?

They should be celebrating that she was alive, but Cassie's words weighed heavy on him. The hesitancy in Naomi's eyes made him see there was definitely more to her rejection of him.

"I should find another place to hide," she said. "You're not responsible for me. I can't put you in this situation of protecting me when you never asked for such trouble."

He moved closer and pulled her close. The sweet smell of her hair drifted up, and her short curls at her temples tickled his nose. He breathed deeply of the sweet, flowery smell. Her forehead fell onto his chest, and for a moment he sensed her yearning for another time.

Or maybe that was him.

He cleared his throat and stepped away. "Let me decide who I protect. I can make up my own mind. I don't need you telling me what I can handle."

She lifted her head and searched his face. A nervous

expression had her swallowing hard. "It's a dangerous world. I don't want anyone to have to handle this."

"That doesn't mean you do it alone. We're heading back, but this time we do this together. You can use Jim's laptop to search, but no more sneaking out. Do you understand?"

"Ya," she replied.

After a moment Sawyer said, "Cassie filled me in on how we're going to keep you safe. It will take some acting skills on our part, but whatever we have to do, we will. I won't let anyone hurt you again. You've endured too much already."

Tears glistened in her eyes as she said, "More than any human being ever should."

TEN

"Did you find anything online?" Sawyer asked from the now-opened doorway to his office in the barn. His shoes hit the wood floorboards with a soft clunk as he stepped inside. Naomi didn't lift her head from the webpage she was on but heard him approach her side. He placed something on the desk beside her, and a quick look out of the corner of her eye showed a tray with red-and-white-checkered cloths over two plates.

"You brought me lunch?" Now she turned and looked up at him. He looked so proud. "How nice of you, but you didn't have to. I was going to take a break soon and help Anna."

He dropped his smile in an instant. "It might be best to wait a few days before getting under her feet. She just needs some time. Once the window is repaired, things will get back to normal."

Naomi frowned. "I'm sure Cassie can find me another place. I don't blame Anna. She has her family to consider."

Sawyer lifted a hand to stop her from saying anything more. "You are welcome here. By us all. No one blames you for what happened here. And Cassie has spread the word that the visitor didn't make it, so no one should be back."

"At least no one knows it was the long-lost Naomi Kemp who didn't make it." She looked back at the screen but didn't see anything through her deep loneliness. "They probably wouldn't have cared anyway."

"Don't say that. Of course people would have. No one wishes ill on you."

"In case you don't remember, someone keeps shooting at me." She touched lightly where the bandage covered her wounds. "I've got the holes to prove it, and Cassie thinks this gunman came from the community. That makes at least two people against me being here."

"Possibly, but that doesn't mean the shooter last night was Amish. He had a car, and I gave Cassie what I saw of the license plate. She may already have a lead, so this whole thing can be put behind you, and you can heal in peace."

"I won't have any peace until Debby's killer is found." Naomi glanced toward the cradle, where little Chloe slept soundly. "I owe her mother that much."

"Why do you owe her?" He pulled up a chair and sat beside her, lifting the cloth napkins from the plates to serve their lunches. "Did she do something for you?"

"No, not anything on purpose, but she allowed me to start again with my work."

"You had to start over at your job? What exactly do you do?" He pushed the laptop back and placed her plate in front of her. A turkey sandwich on rye bread with lettuce and tomato had been cut in half and readied to eat.

Except Naomi's stomach revolted and the idea of

taking one bite was impossible. "I'm not really hungry right now. Maybe the pain meds are messing with my appetite."

"Or the idea of sharing about your life makes you ill. Why all the secrets? Why does your job have to be a secret between us?"

She faced Sawyer in what she hoped was a stern expression of warning. "I'm a social worker. My work is confidential. To protect the women I work with, I can't share about them. And that's all I'm going to say about my job."

"That's a lot of people's secrets to keep. How many can you handle?"

"As many as it takes."

Sawyer took his first bite and chewed slowly. He swallowed and said, "Can you tell me why you think you owe Debby? Is that confidential?"

Naomi pushed her plate away and pulled the laptop back in front of her. She thought of a young woman from the group named Brie Carlson and how she had failed her. Brie had come to the support group a year ago, but one day, she fled a meeting and was hit by a car outside the clinic. She died without healing from her trauma.

"I thought I wasn't cut out for being a social worker." Naomi weighed her words carefully as not to share too much about herself. The key was to keep herself out of her work, and that was something she struggled with. "When you work with traumatized women, it's hard to leave it all at the office. It's hard to know if you've gone too far, or if you didn't go far enough to help someone. That middle ground isn't always clearly seen, and I made a mistake with someone. I lost her, with no way of ever fixing my mistake." Naomi sighed and sent Chloe a sad smile. "I guess, when Debby came to the group, she reminded me I was good at what I did, and it was okay to start again."

Sawyer glanced at the sleeping baby. "Does Chloe have any family who can raise her?"

Naomi shrugged. "Not that I know of. Debby had been in the foster care system growing up. Bumped around a lot, but had no one she called family. I was it for her. From the first day she showed up in group, pregnant and alone, I had to make the decision where my job ended and where our friendship began. I don't regret befriending her. She needed someone to love her, and I'm blessed to have been the one."

Naomi watched Sawyer's light blue eyes begin to sheen as they sat frozen side by side. His compassion came through with the sadness she saw looking back at her.

"Her story is sad, I know," Naomi said. "Tragic, really, and now it gets even sadder as Chloe is an orphan."

"Who had been there for you?" Sawyer's question caught her off guard and she leaned away from him. "After you ran away, I mean," he said. "I always feared you were alone in the world. Please tell me you had someone like Debby had you."

Naomi relaxed at knowing what Sawyer meant. For a moment, she thought he knew about her attack, but that was impossible. "There's a woman who once was Amish who takes in Amish runaways now. I went to her, and she helped me. I worked with her in her store for a while and went to school to earn my diploma. Then took classes at the local college in an accelerated program and eventually earned my degree in social work. She was there to see me graduate. It was nice to have someone there to cheer for me when they called my name. I'll never forget her."

"I'm so glad to hear that. I wondered all the time. If you were safe." He frowned. "We all did."

"Liza." It wasn't a question. Naomi knew that was who he meant. "Believe me when I tell you I never wanted—"

"I know." Sawyer took her hands in his and forced her to face him head on. "I know, Naomi."

Words that should have offered her peace gave her an uneasy feeling and a growing fear. Once again, she questioned what exactly he knew. Shame resurfaced in an instant and panic had her heart rate speeding up. The physical response was unfounded. He didn't know anything. Only what she had willingly and carefully shared.

Unless Cassie...

No. Naomi shook the thought away. She was just being paranoid. The sheriff wouldn't break confidentiality. She was subject to the same protocol as Naomi was in her field of work.

"Liza never doubted you. I wish I could say the same, but that would be a lie."

Naomi breathed a sigh of relief. He was talking about Liza, not himself. "I don't deserve Liza's loyalty," Naomi blurted out. "I hurt her too. I hurt so many in leaving. You, Liza, my parents…the whole community. If I could only go back and do that night over again."

Sawyer gently rubbed her hand, offering the comfort

of touch. A feeling she'd long forgotten spread out from where he made contact to warm her entire body. She closed her eyes to cherish the memory of long ago. A time when they had a lifetime to look forward to with each other.

"So much was lost that night," Sawyer whispered sadly.

Naomi could only nod. He felt the loss too, of what might have been. What was supposed to have been.

Sawyer and Naomi, *mann* and *fraa.*

"I want nothing more than to go back to that night and change what happened to…us."

Naomi slipped her hand from his grasp and held it in her lap. "It's not possible, Sawyer. I'm not the same girl you knew. I can't be the woman you think I am. That Naomi Kemp is gone forever."

"Because you like being English," he said.

Naomi bit her lower lip. It was the easiest reason to give, but she couldn't make herself lie. She'd never fit into the English world and so she'd accepted hers would be a life of singlehood. Helping the women at the clinic brought her the joy she needed to have as full a life as possible. "I have a rewarding job where I am needed. It's what I want. It's what I need."

He let out a deep sigh and pulled his hand away.

"*Ya*, I'm glad to hear you found what you were looking for. I wouldn't give up my time with Liza for anything either. In a sense, I have you to thank for our marriage. It was short, but beautiful. I'm sorry if that hurts you, but you should know—"

"No," Naomi cut him off. "It doesn't." She huffed a short laugh. "Surprisingly, it actually makes me happy to know something good came out of that night. You were able to be a wonderful husband to Liza. I'm glad to know she had this before she…" Naomi swallowed hard. The idea of her dear friend's life cut short didn't seem real. It didn't seem fair. "I'm glad she wasn't alone. I'm glad she had…" Naomi raised her gaze to Sawyer. "You."

Sawyer frowned, then ran his palms across his black pants. "I'll be honest. Liza was a loving wife, but I fear I fell short as her *mann*. The business consumed me. Maybe if I hadn't been so busy, I would have noticed her getting sick sooner."

"Going back isn't an option. That goes the same for you." Naomi smirked, then smiled big when she saw she'd made her point.

"Then from here on out, we only go forward, *ya*?"

"*Ya.*"

Sawyer nodded at the laptop. "Starting with what you've been searching. Care to share?"

The screen stood still on a social media website. Multiple accounts with the same name lined the page.

Sawyer leaned close and read the name. "Irving Adams. Who's that?"

Naomi pressed her lips together, then spoke in a rush. "It's probably nothing, but Debby talked in her sleep. She spoke this man's name a few times. She had met a man on a dating website. He…" Naomi stopped abruptly and cleared her throat. Could she share a bit of Debby's story? Should she?

Sawyer covered her hand, and she realized she was trembling. "Take your time. I'm not going anywhere."

Naomi locked her gaze on where his hand held hers,

so gently. So patiently. She let out a deep sigh and said, "Debby was date-raped." Naomi looked Chloe's way. "Her attacker is Chloe's father."

"Irving Adams?" Sawyer frowned and his cheek ticked. The news seemed to shake him a bit. He averted his gaze and studied the numerous pictures of men named Irving Adams on the laptop's screen.

Naomi followed his direction to the screen too. "I can only guess on his name. That she never shared, except maybe in her sleep."

After a few moments of silence, Sawyer said, "I'm sorry that happened to your friend. But didn't she want to press charges?"

Naomi was glad he was looking at the computer screen. The way she worried her lower lip could make him see more than she wanted him to. "Many victims are shamed into keeping quiet. They don't report the crime because of fear and because they feel they are to blame. By the time Debby came to the support group, weeks had gone by, and…" Naomi looked to the cradle.

"And she knew she was with child," Sawyer finished the sentence.

"She feared her attacker would find out about the baby and hurt her again. And hurt the baby."

Sawyer studied the names on the screen. "So let's start with the first one and go down the list. I don't know much about computers. Jim handles all things technical, but I can read through each account to see if any of the Irving Adams lived in or near Kentucky. Maybe there will only be one. That will for certain sure narrow down the list."

For the next hour, the two of them went through each

account and cross-checked the names with addresses listed online. By the time they checked the last Irving on the list, it was safe to say there was only one Irving Adams in the state. But judging by his personal photos, he seemed to be a happily married man with three children and a successful law firm in Louisville.

"Are you sure this is the guy?" Sawyer asked. "He doesn't seem like the type."

"There is no type. We should look through everything first." Naomi opened an album of pictures on Irving's page and scrolled through them slowly. Most pictures were of his wife and his children. A few had him in them and showcased a close, loving family with a big dog and an expansive home. "He does have an abundant life, but that doesn't mean he's innocent."

"Why risk all this?" Sawyer said. "I still don't think this is the right guy."

Naomi closed the album and clicked on Irving Adams's list of followers. A few scrolls down, and Naomi let out a crying shout, then covered her mouth.

"What's wrong? What do you see?"

"Not what." She pointed her finger at a picture of her friend. "Who. That's Debby. He knew Debby."

Just then, Chloe let out a soft cry that transformed into something much louder and angry. Naomi stood to get the baby from an unfinished hope chest Sawyer had been building in his workshop. As she gave comfort to the waking child, she noticed Sawyer had yet to take his eyes off the album of pictures.

"What are you looking at?" Naomi asked as she bounced the screaming baby at her shoulder.

"The baby in this picture looks familiar."

He slowly turned and looked at Naomi.

No, not at her but at Chloe.

He pointed at the screen. "I'd say that's Chloe, but this image is at least three years old. It can't be her."

The baby screamed louder. Naomi held her tighter, murmuring soothing sounds to calm her. With her gaze locked on the baby in the picture, she approached the screen to get a better look. It did look like Chloe.

Or Chloe's sister.

"It's him," she said in shock. "We found Debby's rapist."

Sawyer jumped to his feet and took the crying child from her arms. He brought Chloe to his shoulder and tucked her close into the warmth of his neck. His large hands practically covered her body. Chloe immediately calmed in his arms and all looked peaceful in this paternal image. *Boppli* and *daedi*.

Except Sawyer wasn't Chloe's father.

The man on the screen was.

Over Chloe's nestled body, he gave her the most somber face she had ever seen on him. "If that's her rapist, then he's also her killer."

"And he's trying to erase all evidence," Naomi said and looked to the innocent baby in his arms.

Sawyer tucked Chloe tighter. "I will not let him. I promise you. I will guard her with my life. And you too."

Naomi sat in the rocking chair in the living room giving Chloe her bottle, taking in the baby's tiny fists as she gripped it with enthusiasm.

"She's hungry," Sawyer's nephew, Ben, said as he

peered over Naomi's shoulder to watch. "I've never seen a baby eat like that. She might eat the whole bottle."

Naomi chuckled. "That would be something to see. Do you want to feed her?"

The little boy's eyes lit up in delight, and he nodded his head.

Naomi stood, careful not to disturb the hungry infant from her food. "Hop up," she instructed the boy. When Ben had readied himself on the rocker and raised his arms, she placed the baby in his lap and showed him how to hold her safely. "I'll hold the bottle until you feel comfortable."

"I'm comfortable. Let me do it," he said with a bit of a whine.

"Okay, keep one arm around the baby to support her, and with your other hand, hold the bottle where I am. That's it. Keep it tilted up, so she can eat. You got it!" Naomi beamed at the child, but she still stayed low and close.

"I am doing it. *Mamm*, look!" Ben called to Anna in the kitchen. She had her back to them as she prepped tonight's dinner. "Watch me, *Mamm*!"

Anna angled her head and gave a short nod. She looked to Naomi but turned away quickly. "Nice work, Ben. You'll be helping with all the babies in the community soon."

"Did you hear that, Naomi?" Ben whispered in awe. "I'm going to get to help with the babies."

"You'll be wonderful at it. Look," Naomi whispered back. "Chloe is already falling asleep. Your feeding filled her right up."

"Can you take her now? I want to go play. I left my horse on the front porch."

Naomi took Chloe from his arms, and the boy raced off for something more exciting than a sleeping baby.

"I'll just bring her upstairs to her cradle," Naomi told the back of Anna. When no response came from her, Naomi left quietly through the hall toward the front of the house.

Sawyer came through the front door with a tool in his hand. He stopped at the foot of the stairs when he saw her coming. A soft smile spread across his face as she drew closer.

"I'm going to bring her upstairs," Naomi whispered when she stood directly in front of him. He had to step back to allow her to pass.

But he didn't.

"Is everything all right?" she asked.

He looked down at the sweet, peaceful expression on Chloe's plump face. "Everything's...perfect." A few beats extended out as he studied the infant in her arms. Then he looked back at Naomi. His smile slowly faded. Then he whispered, "Nearly."

She cleared her throat and insinuated she needed to get by, and he quickly caught on and stepped back to allow her to pass to the stairs. Naomi made her way up, unmistakably aware of him watching her ascend the steps. She quickly disappeared into her room.

Once she laid Chloe in her cradle, Naomi took the moment to tuck a wayward curl back under her prayer *kapp* and press her hands down the front of her purple dress. She glanced down to be sure Chloe hadn't left any messy burps on her shoulders before she made her way back downstairs.

As she descended, she saw Sawyer fixing the newel post at the base of the staircase. She remembered how the knob had fallen off when she'd sneaked out a few nights ago. The night she'd nearly died.

She whispered as she hit the last step, "I owe that newel my life."

Sawyer raised an eyebrow. "How so?"

"It's what alerted the household to me sneaking outside. If it hadn't fallen off, I wouldn't have made such a clatter, and no one would have woken up. I might be dead now."

Sawyer looked at the round wood piece in his hands with wide eyes. "This is what woke me up?" He lifted it off the post and gave it a quick kiss.

Naomi laughed and quickly covered her mouth so as not to wake the baby. But her laughter died when she heard the sound of a buggy's wheels turning down the driveway outside.

Sawyer also put the forgotten newel back on its post to check out the screen door. "We have company. Quick, back upstairs and don't come out until they're gone. I'll do my best to hurry them. If they ask for an invite to dinner, you won't be able to come down. Understand?"

"Who is it?" Naomi asked and she leaned to see out the screen too.

"None of your concern. You only need to worry about staying alive, and that means staying out of sight. Now, go." He pointed up the stairs and he picked up his tool and pushed open the screen.

Naomi's last sight of him was his back as he stepped

onto the porch to wait for the buggy to come to a complete stop. With a quick turn, she hurried up the stairs and to her room. Closing the door with a soft click, she raced to the window and stood off to the side, hoping for a glimpse of the visitor. A few moments later, she had her way, but jolted back against the wall when she saw who climbed down from the buggy.

"*Mamm* and *Daed*," she whispered. Why were her parents here?

Through the open window, her father's gruff voice drifted up from below. Instant tears pricked her eyes. For eight years, she'd thought she would never hear their voices again. She listened for her mother's and closed her eyes when Maggie Kemp joined her husband, Daniel, in greeting Sawyer at the steps.

The front screen door opened, and Naomi heard Anna join them outside.

Naomi leaned close to the window and sought out a view of her parents. She could make out the top of her *daed*'s black brimmed hat and his shoulders, but from this view above, she couldn't see his face. She leaned another way to try for something, anything. She just wanted to see them again, even from afar.

"We've gotten word that your visitor was shot and didn't make it," Daniel said solemnly, taking his hat off to hold in front of him.

Naomi inhaled sharply, delighted that she could see her father clearly now. She reached a hand down to him, wanting to touch his beard, now so much whiter than she remembered. He looked so much older.

How much have I missed?

The question swirled around in her mind, drowning out the conversation going on down below.

"Fannie told us it was her." Maggie spoke with pain in her voice, pulling Naomi's attention to her mother. She tried to piece the conversation together and listened intently.

"I'm sorry, but Fannie was never told any such thing. She shouldn't have bothered you with this," Sawyer said. "She will need to be corrected. Anna will be sure to talk to her right away. Right, Anna?"

Anna spoke quickly. "I'll talk to her today. I'm sorry she caused you both such pain."

"So your visitor wasn't Naomi? She wasn't our daughter?" Daniel demanded brusquely.

At Sawyer's hesitation, Maggie broke down into tears and Anna ran down the steps to comfort her. "Sawyer, do something," she ordered her brother to put an end to this charade.

But the sheriff was adamant about no one knowing she was here and sticking with the story that the visitor died of a gunshot wound. To tell the Kemps the truth could put Naomi in immediate danger again. It could put them in danger if the shooter or shooters went after them to get to her. Naomi understood the risks of breaking her promise to Cassie, but she still opened her mouth to yell down to them. She wanted them to know she was alive. She wanted them to invite her back into their fold.

But that would never happen.

The truth stole the air from her lungs and the gumption she had a moment before to break her promise.

"I'm sorry, Daniel," Sawyer said sadly. "All information will need to come from Sheriff Shaw."

"Please," Maggie cried. "Please just say yes or no, so we can finally mourn the loss of our daughter. Is she…dead?"

Sawyer spoke in a low tone that Naomi could barely hear. She leaned forward and turned an ear as he said, "All I can say, Maggie, is… You've already mourned the loss of your daughter. You don't need to mourn her twice."

Maggie continued to weep, and her husband wrapped an arm around her and led her back to the buggy. The two climbed aboard and silently departed with no goodbyes exchanged. As soon as the buggy disappeared from view, footsteps stomped up the inside staircase and the door to her room burst open.

A flushed Sawyer stood in the doorway, his heavy breathing lifting and dropping his shoulders rapidly. He lifted his arms, whether to invite her in to comfort her or out of anguish for what just happened below, she didn't care. All Naomi wanted was to be held by them.

She left the window in a dash and barreled at him full force. Raising her arms, she wrapped them around his neck as though he was the only thing that would keep her from drowning in despair. His arms enveloped her securely and lifted her off the floor in a tight embrace. Her feet swung in the air.

"I'm sorry," he whispered into the side of her head. He pushed his face against her ear. "I couldn't lie, and I couldn't tell the truth. I didn't want to break the Commandment."

"I wouldn't want you to either," she said frantically.

She might have turned away from God, but to have Sawyer make such a break seemed all wrong. But everything felt wrong about today. Her parents should be beside her through all this. But that was impossible. "I wanted to yell down so much. I nearly did. But I knew nothing would change, and I could put them in danger too."

"I wasn't expecting them to come here. I didn't know Fannie went to them. I should have thought of this. I should have prepared for them."

Naomi shook her head. "It's not your fault. I already hurt them. This is all my fault for ever bringing this pain on them in the first place."

"You did nothing wrong." Sawyer spoke against her ear, then pulled back and lowered her feet to the floor. He took her face into his hands and looked directly into her eyes. "You did nothing wrong. Do you hear me? Nothing."

"You keep saying things like this, but you don't understand." Naomi tried to avert her gaze, but he held her face still.

"Then tell me. You don't think I can handle the truth, but I'm telling you I can. Trust me."

Hope sprouted deep within her. Did she dare tell him her darkest secret? What the biggest mistake in her life led her to?

Naomi opened her mouth but quickly closed it, shutting in even one syllable of her secret. She couldn't bear seeing the disgust on his face. She couldn't handle him telling her, "I told you so." It had been him who tried to convince her not to go to that party. He would have every right to say it.

"I—I…can't."

A crestfallen expression crossed his face. He couldn't understand, but it was best he didn't know. It was not his burden to carry. His beautiful blue eyes met hers. "When you're ready, I'm here."

"And if I'm never ready? Will you still be there for me?"

His silence told her he wouldn't be able to have this between them forever. Eventually, he would walk away for good.

The sound of car tires crunching the gravel of the driveway reached up through the bedroom window and saved him from answering her. Sawyer dropped his hands to his sides and stepped around her for the window.

He visibly relaxed. "Just my partner. I've got some work to do in the barn with him." He turned back to her and smiled at the sleeping baby as he did. "Will the two of you be all right up here while I work?"

"Of course, go." Naomi stepped out of the way of the door to encourage him to leave. "You have a business to run. It can't stop on my account."

"It *will* stop if it comes between you and Chloe's safety. No piece of furniture is worth a life." Sawyer left the room and headed downstairs. She watched him from the window meet a man in a cowboy hat. Naomi did a double take at the hat, remembering the hat the first shooter had worn.

Could it be?

Naomi scoffed at the thought. This was horse country. Practically every household had a cowboy hat in it somewhere.

Still, she studied the man as he stepped from his car and shook Sawyer's hand. They laughed about something and went into the barn side by side.

Sawyer had told her he had an English partner but seeing him with one so casually made her wonder if maybe he would consider leaving the Amish.

Another blossom of hope burst up from her midriff, and she wrapped an arm around the place jumping with butterflies. She couldn't let the hope of a future with Sawyer take root. To ask such a thing of him would be wrong. It would be blasphemous. He was a baptized member of the church, sworn to uphold the Amish way of life and *ordnung*. She was cutoff and now an outsider.

Chloe stirred from her nap and let out a whimper. Naomi reached into the cradle and rubbed her tiny back as she woke up to being comforted by the closest thing to a mother she had.

"If I could be your mom, I would," Naomi said, glancing out the window beyond the billowing curtains. "Just like if I could be his wife, I would." She sighed and scooped up the baby into her arms. She kissed the smiling child on the nose. "But neither are possible, so for now, I'll be a friend to you both…for however long that lasts."

Naomi let the hope for that to be a long time take root, even though an uneasy feeling came over her. A dreaded feeling of danger loomed, threatening to cut her time with both Chloe and Sawyer short.

Maybe even permanently.

ELEVEN

"When you said things had been harrowing around here, I just thought you meant business was hopping," Jim said from the desk and flashed his cracked tooth in a grin. He typed on the laptop as he pulled down this week's online orders. "I had no idea you meant criminal. I'm sorry to hear you all have had to deal with such danger. I was shocked when I heard your guest was killed. That's horrible. Any idea who shot her?"

Sawyer didn't respond as he sanded the gun cabinet, doing what he did best while Jim did what he did best—computers.

Suddenly, it hit Sawyer. Maybe Jim could track down where Irving Adams lived. "No, but there is a man who might be involved. Perhaps you would know how to find him. His name is Irving Adams. I found him on a social media site, but I don't have a home address for him. Somewhere in Louisville is all I know."

"And you want *my* help?" Jim asked over the screen.

"It would mean a lot if you could help. You know I'm not supposed to be using technology. That's why I brought you on with the business. But I understand this task is above and beyond your duties, so if you would rather not be involved—"

"No, not a problem. Of course I want to help you any way I can. Count me in. Anything to catch a killer, especially a killer of an Amish woman. That's just shameful to go after a woman of such simple living. What kind of sick person would hurt such a soft-natured individual? I'm surprised she didn't run away the first time he came after her."

Sawyer frowned, thinking of Naomi's first flight eight years ago. Had someone else hurt Naomi? Could that be what had made her run? He dropped his head and rubbed his forehead.

"Hey, Sawyer, I'm sorry about this Amish woman. She obviously meant something to you for you to be this upset."

Sawyer lifted his gaze to his friend and partner, a bit stumped at Jim's words. But he wasn't far off. "A long time ago, yes, but not anymore."

"So you knew her?"

Sawyer realized his slip instantly. No one was supposed to know it was Naomi Kemp who had come back.

Jim stood up with pleading hands outstretched, palms up. "Sorry, Sawyer. I didn't mean to pry or put you on the spot. You can trust me not to say a thing to anyone. And of course, I will help you look into this Adams guy. You need something, you name it."

"Thank you, Jim." Sawyer relaxed. With his partner not knowing very many of the Amish in town, there really was no reason to be concerned that word would spread.

"When will the authorities release the woman's name?" Jim asked.

Lying wasn't possible for him, but Sawyer wondered how long he could go on saying he didn't know anything before people called him out. Every time someone asked him a question, he sought for the simplest choice of words that wouldn't lock him in to a bald-faced lie. "The truth will come out soon," he said, careful not to sway in either direction, to remain indifferent. "It's an ongoing investigation," Sawyer said and went back to his work on the gun case. *Please, Jim, just drop it*, he silently pleaded as his sanding grew louder with each stroke. "I should have this done for you next week," he said, attempting to change the subject.

"Perfect timing," Jim said after a long hesitation. He closed the laptop and scooped up the handful of new orders to put into the project bin. "But work on these first. Real customers first. It's not even hunting season yet. At least not for deer. I can wait. I'm patient." He chuckled and walked up behind Sawyer.

Sawyer glanced over his shoulder to see Jim running a hand up the edge of the gun case, where a knot in the wood was visible. "The glass door will go over that. You won't even see it."

"I'm not complaining. It gives it character. The whole piece is beautiful. I'm going to have to buy more guns to fill it." He chuckled. "Not that my brother will mind."

"Do you both hunt a lot?" Sawyer asked and went on sanding.

"My whole family does. It's a family affair, I guess you could say. Passed down from generations before.

Hunting is a way of life for us, and we never miss our shot."

Sawyer slowed the sanding and finally came to a stop. He glanced up to see Jim staring out the window at the house.

"If you're not able to help find Irving Adams, it's okay," Sawyer said, snapping Jim's attention from the house back to him.

"It's no problem. I told you I will help in whatever way I can. I'll get right on that search and be back here as soon as possible. Maybe even by tomorrow." He headed to the door. "Do you think Anna has any of her banana bread made already? I think I'll knock on the door and see if she'll take pity on this old bachelor and give me some."

Sawyer jumped to his feet, his heart racing. He dropped the sandpaper to the floor. "I'll get you some." He rushed to the door. "Forgive my rudeness. I know she always has something for you. I should have brought it out to you."

"Sawyer, calm down. I can get it. Besides, I never get to say hello to the baker herself. She usually sends it to the shop. Now's my chance to greet her and thank her appropriately."

Sawyer did his best to be nonchalant when he fell in line beside Jim and walked with him out the barn and toward the house. "I think she made a nut bread today," he said a little too loudly, hoping someone heard him through the opened windows as he neared. "Anna will be glad to give you something to go."

Sawyer prayed she heard and would meet him at the

door. He also prayed Naomi and Chloe remained upstairs and out of sight.

As they hit the first step, Sawyer yelled, "Anna, Jim's here to say hi. He hopes you have a sweet treat for him today."

Jim laughed loudly. "Sawyer, you're making me sound like a good-for-nothing leech." He reached for the screen door's handle.

Sawyer forced a smile as his breathing hitched and tightened in his chest. He made a grab for the handle first, but Jim beat him to it.

Then the baby let out a loud cry that echoed through the house. Jim looked through the screen and up the stairs in the direction it came.

"That baby doesn't sound happy," he said and dropped his hand from the handle. "Maybe now's not the time to disrupt Anna. I didn't realize she had another baby. How about I take a raincheck for when I get you that information?"

Sawyer let out a deep sigh. "That sounds fine with me. I'll be sure to have something ready for you."

The men said their goodbyes, and Sawyer watched as Jim climbed into his car and backed up. Sawyer's gaze fell to the license plate and a quick read of a certain group of numbers caught his attention.

8-3-8-3-1-7.

The *3-8-3-1* were the same as the car that nearly ran him over in the dark the other night. He had thought the plate began with a *B* and ended in a *2. Could he have been wrong? Were they really an* 8 *and a* 7?

But that would mean it was Jim's car.

The screen door behind him opened, and he jolted at the sound.

"What has gotten into you?" Anna stood there with a towel, drying her hands.

"Sorry," Sawyer said and took off his hat to rub a hand through his hair and push his thoughts away. He reached for the door to come in for dinner. "This plan to keep Naomi's presence here a secret is harder than I realized. It has my nerves stretched to their limits. I'll be glad when this is all over."

Anna huffed and pursed her lips. "You know what to do, *brudder*. If you had listened to me this would already be over."

After two more days of the silent treatment from Anna, Naomi scooped up Chloe and headed out to the barn. Careful to stay out of view of the street, in case someone happened to be passing by, she stuck to the trees and picked up her pace in the open portion of the trek. She entered through the back door of the barn, directly into Sawyer's workshop. She slammed the door behind her and fell back against it.

"I don't know how much longer I can smile through Anna's torment," she told him. "Maybe you should let her arrange a blind date for you. That would make her happy again. What do you say?"

Sawyer slowly lifted his head up from a table he was staining. His lack of humor spoke for him. "I thought you were my friend."

Naomi smiled and hiked Chloe up farther on her hip. "I am. *We* are, aren't we, Chloe?" Naomi bopped the baby on the nose. The child's eyes crossed just before she burst out in the most adorable belly laugh.

Naomi laughed with the baby in a contagious way, and before she knew it, all three of them were joining in the merriment. Naomi repeated the nose bop, and Chloe laughed even harder. Minutes went by before she sighed her last giggle and beamed joyful eyes up at Naomi.

In awe at this child's complete trust in her, tears pricked Naomi's eyes. "Oh, Sawyer, she's so perfect. I never knew a baby could make me feel this way. So complete. So purposeful." Naomi smiled at the baby's sweet face, then glanced up to see Sawyer's serious one watching her across the table.

She felt her lips twitch as they locked eyes on each other. Then the smile became harder to keep. She let it drift away as he slowly wound around the furniture and ambled in a slow, direct line to her, never taking his gaze from her.

He wore no hat, and his hair was flat from being squashed by it earlier. It gave him the look of the little boy's innocence she remembered from their childhood. But Sawyer was no longer a child.

And neither was she.

"When you showed up here with Chloe, I thought you lacked natural motherly instincts. I actually felt bad for the baby."

"I'm trying my best," Naomi said in her own defense.

Sawyer shook his head in all seriousness.

"I'm not?" Her voice cracked.

"Chloe would be blessed to have you as her *mamm*. I've watched how you care for her so selflessly and lovingly. She adores you and trusts you and follows you around the room with her eyes. You are everything to her."

"But I'm not her mother, and you are right, I do lack the skills to be anyone's mother. I'm totally winging this, and I know I'm failing miserably."

"Who says?"

"Well, you just did. And Anna reminds me constantly with her disgusted looks at everything I do."

Displeasure crossed his face. "First, I need to apologize for myself. I know I didn't treat you any better than Anna does when you first came back. I was wrong. And so is she. You are doing an amazing job with Chloe. Please believe that. And in a second, I'm going to go talk with Anna and put an end to this desire she has to make your time here so miserable. There's no cause for this treatment."

"No, Sawyer, it's fine. I can handle it. I can take whatever she throws at me. I'm tough."

Sawyer smirked. "That you are." His eyes turned sad in the next instant, and his lips thinned into a slight frown.

"Is everything all right?" she asked.

He searched her eyes for a few moments of silence before he said, "People get stronger by enduring hardships or...by traumatic incidences. In your line of work, you must know that."

Naomi frowned and nodded once, not knowing where he was going with this. "Sometimes."

"Right, because sometimes they run. Like you did."

Naomi swallowed hard. She held Chloe close as though the baby could guard her from his questions.

"Why did you go into your line of work, Naomi?"

"I told you already. Because I'm good at what I do." Her response came out in a rush.

"Because you can relate to these women?" So did his.

Naomi had no response for him. All she could do was shake her head back and forth as though that would put an end to this line of questioning.

"Did something happen to you?"

Naomi felt the blood drain from her face. Her head pounded as his question echoed inside her mind. "That's enough, Sawyer." She spoke forcefully. "You don't know what you're doing. Don't say another word."

Sawyer listened to her, but even his silence spoke volumes.

He knew. He might not know the details, but he knew something happened to her.

But how?

Chloe cooed and gurgled in the heavy silence. Then she let out a cry. She had enough of being ignored. Her outburst effectively broke the connection and Sawyer pulled away a few inches.

He said, "Someone's wanting some attention. All right, little one. You're coming with me. Time for a diaper change, I'd say." He scooped up the baby from Naomi's arms and looked over Chloe's back at her. "I'll be back soon. I'm going to talk to Anna too. Things are going to change here for you. For us both."

"Nothing can ever change." He needed to know the Amish life could never be an option for her again. She was not about to tell everyone why she really left.

In the next second, he turned his back and left through the door to go back to the house, chatting sweetly to the baby in his arms as though Naomi's words meant nothing. His voice lingered through the barn and grew faint as he walked on.

This was dangerous ground they were on. The faster Sheriff Shaw found Irving Adams, and whoever else is hunting her, the faster Naomi could return to her life.

Alone.

But alone meant without Chloe…and without Sawyer. It would feel like it had eight years ago when she didn't have anyone.

But that wasn't true. She now had her career, and she had her group. She wouldn't be alone like before. She would be okay.

Once she was safe again, she would be okay.

A crunching footstep in the barn alerted her to Sawyer coming back. "I meant what I said," she said to the open doorway. But it wasn't Sawyer who appeared at the door in the next moment.

Across the workshop, the man with the cowboy hat who had visited Sawyer a couple days ago stepped inside. He removed his hat as a slow, lopsided smile spread on his lips. "I knew it," he said. "You ain't dead. You ain't dead, at all. Hello, Naomi." He flashed a wide grin, exposing a chipped tooth. "Remember me?"

TWELVE

The night of the party flashed in her eyes. Snippets and scenes always played on repeat at the back of her mind, but no matter how hard she tried to elongate them, to gather more of the details, she never could. But the sight of this man's chipped tooth did what no amount of therapy could.

It gave her another scene.

The after scene.

"James Clark. You helped me," she said.

"Yes, but please, call me Jim. James is so formal, and after what we shared that night so long ago, I would say it made us friends, wouldn't you?" He took slow steps toward her.

Jim? Sawyer's friend Jim was the James she remembered? She gave a half-committed nod while putting that together.

"Oh, come on, you had been knocked unconscious and left by the trash outside. I needed to get you out of there. It wasn't safe for you. I took care of you, didn't I? You shouldn't have been there in the first place."

"I know." The lasting guilt would always plague her.

She told her women in the support group that allowing the shame to continue would never allow them to see the truth. But letting it go was harder than one thought. "My mind always wonders, what if I had listened to Sawyer? Or what if I had stayed home with my friend who backed out?"

"Yes, things would have been so much better for you." He stood beside a table Sawyer had been staining, only a few feet from her now. "Why did you come back?"

"I had to find someplace safe," she said. "I thought Rogues Ridge would be it."

"You thought wrong." His quick response came with an edge that raised the hair on the back of Naomi's neck. She shifted her stance nervously. This was Sawyer's friend, and the man who had helped her eight years ago. There was no reason to fear him.

Was there?

She swallowed hard on a parched throat. "Why was I wrong in coming back here?"

"Because you had done so much to move on from here. To get past what happened that night."

Suddenly, Naomi wondered if Jim had told Sawyer about that night. Did Sawyer know about her attack? Fear spread through her at the thought, but she had to know. "When you helped me, you promised not to tell anyone," she said. "I didn't want Sawyer knowing."

The man raised his hands. "Hey, if he knows, it didn't come from me. Honest."

Naomi relaxed a bit. "Are you sure he doesn't know?"

"Beats me. All I know is I got you out of town that

night. Brought you to that motel to get cleaned up. I even paid for the room, remember?"

Naomi nodded, but that night was a blur. "I remember being dropped off at Edna's, the ex-Amish woman who helps Amish runaways. Did you bring me there?"

"Sure, the next day. I did that for you. And then we parted ways, and I promised to not tell anyone where you were. And I didn't."

"Why did you go to work for Sawyer?" she asked.

"He needed a website technician. It's what I do. I handle a lot of sites for the town, and even the state. That's all."

The answer seemed legitimate, but knowing how close the two men worked still made her uneasy.

"Look, I just came by to give Sawyer some information he had asked me for. I didn't mean to startle you." Jim removed a folded-up piece of paper from his jeans pocket. "He wanted the address of a man named Irving Adams."

She locked her eyes on the paper as he passed it over to her, but she couldn't take it.

Debby's killer's information had been all she wanted. Now she just wanted to be free from it all. To not look Sawyer in the eye again, in case he knew everything.

"That should go to Sheriff Shaw," she said.

Jim shrugged. "That's fine. Do you want to take it to her?" He reached into his back pocket and withdrew a key ring. "You can take my car, if you want. I'll help you any way I can. Just like I did before."

Now he held both out to her. This man had come to her aid once before, in her darkest hour, and it appeared he was again.

Slowly, Naomi stepped away from the door that had backed her up to this point. She took a steady step closer to him. Then another. She reached a hand to take the paper first. She grasped it, but he didn't relinquish it. She tugged once, then looked up from the paper to see his chipped tooth in a grin.

"Why are you so nervous? Relax," he said. Then he let the paper go.

She curled it into the palm of her hand and reached for the key ring.

"What's going on?" Sawyer barked from the doorway, and immediately Naomi jumped back a few steps.

Jim turned away from Naomi to face Sawyer, who walked toward them. "Jim, you shouldn't be in here."

"I'm sorry. I came by to give you that address you asked me for. I just gave it to Naomi. I was about to give her my car key as well, so she could bring the information I found to the sheriff." Jim laughed nervously. "You had me going there. I was a bit shocked to see her alive."

Sawyer directed his next question to Naomi. "Are you all right?"

She nodded, averting her gaze to the floor beside him.

"Can I see that?" he asked and reached for the paper.

Naomi let it go. He unfolded it and read it silently. "This is more than I asked for." He looked at Jim. "How did you get all this information?"

Jim scoffed and grinned. "I've got a little brother in with the bigwigs in the state. You know that. He can track anyone down. He can track their dog down too."

Sawyer looked to Naomi. "Jim's family are politicians," he said as though she'd asked.

She shrugged her indifference and said, "I don't follow politics all that much. Sorry. You must be proud."

Jim grinned a big and bright chipped-tooth smile. "My brother's got his eye on a US Senate seat, and I mean to do everything I can to get him there. Helping people is what I do best." He winked her way.

Her breath hitched. She glanced at Sawyer, but he didn't see it.

Sawyer waved a hand to encompass the workshop. "That you do. You help me daily with the business. I can barely keep up with the orders since you came on board to handle the internet store. You make big things happen, and I know your brother is good as gold with you by his side."

So he hadn't seen the wink. Naomi sighed and nodded to the piece of paper. "I just want to get that to Cassie right away."

"I can take it into town tomor—" Sawyer said.

"No," she cut him off. "Now. I can drive James's— I mean Jim's car."

"Where is your car?" Sawyer asked him. "I didn't see it out there. I didn't even know you were here."

"I pulled it up alongside the barn. It's out there." He held the keys back out to Naomi. "Go ahead, take them. I'll walk home. I'm not too far. I loan it out a lot. Return it when you don't need it anymore. I've got my truck. It's the least I can do to help you both."

Naomi stepped forward again, but this time when she reached for the keys, Jim relinquished them right away.

Sawyer stepped close to Naomi and said, "Jim, we

need your secrecy about Naomi being here. If anyone asks, you can't tell them you saw her."

"Of course, you've got my word. Naomi knows I won't tell a soul, right, Naomi?" Jim asked her directly.

She squirmed a bit under his insinuation, hoping Sawyer wouldn't ask questions. She nodded and said, "He won't tell."

Sawyer eyed them both back and forth, but if he had any concerns, he held his tongue. Instead, he turned to Naomi as he asked, "Are you okay with driving? It's getting dark, so no one should see you, but if you would rather not go, I'm sure Jim would take me."

"I'm going," Naomi said. "I want to talk to the sheriff…privately."

Sawyer nodded. "Are you sure we can't drop you off somewhere, Jim?"

"Nope, you two go ahead." Jim headed toward the door. Before he exited, he glanced back and made a zipping sound, pretending to zip his lips shut. "Your secret is safe with me." He looked Naomi's way, and she knew he meant the first secret of that night long ago.

When he was gone, she let out a deep sigh of relief.

"Why do I feel like there was more going on than the two of you said? It's almost as if you two knew each other already." Sawyer folded the paper back up and slipped it into his pants pocket. "Did you?"

"Can we just go? The faster Cassie finds these shooters, the faster I can get out of this town."

Sawyer flinched and his mouth dropped open in surprise. He recovered quickly and said, "What about Chloe?"

Could she leave without saying goodbye to the baby?

If she had known the last time she held Chloe and laughed with her was their final time together, she would have held her tighter. No. She wouldn't have let her go. *It's best this way.* "Why don't you stay here with her? Take care of her," Naomi said somberly. "I can go by myself."

Sawyer grew quiet. He studied her in the fading daylight, and she could tell he knew she did not plan to return.

"Goodbye, Sawyer," Naomi whispered and walked toward the side of the barn where Jim said he'd parked the car.

"Wait." Sawyer followed her to the car, but after she got in and held her hand out for the paper, he kept it from her. "What happened in there? What did Jim say to make you run again? Did he hurt you?"

"He never hurt me. He helped me to see I shouldn't have come back."

Naomi reached for the car door to pull it closed. Surprisingly, Sawyer backed away to let her, but he quickly ran around the back and had the passenger door open before she could stop him. He climbed in and shut the door. "You can push me away all you want, but I'm not letting you run away again."

The car moved through the winding roads abutting the cliffs that Rogues Ridge was named for. With no streetlights out in the country, the only guides were those of the car's headlights and the red interior lights that cast bouncing shadows on Naomi's face as she drove.

She'd yet to say a word since he jumped in the car

and demanded to go with her. He could tell by the way she worried her lower lip she was planning something.

"Don't even think you're going to lose me," he said. "I meant what I said. No more running."

"It's not running if I have a life to go back to. It's called going home."

"You already came home," he replied. "You came back home. With Chloe. Could you really leave her behind?"

Remorse squeezed her heart and she shook her head. "I wouldn't have been able to. But I need to return to the women in my group. Rogues Ridge doesn't feel like home to me anymore. The Amish life is over for me. I have a job where people are depending on me. I've lost two women now. I have to get back to the others."

"What do you mean you lost two? There's another besides Debby?" He heard his voice raise and took a breath to control his shock. "Does the sheriff know?"

"Brie's death has nothing to do with Debby, but yes, I told her I'd lost another woman to a hit-and-run."

Sawyer bit down hard and looked out the passenger window. He reined in his emotions, knowing getting upset wouldn't help her trust him more. But something felt wrong. Deadly wrong. "When did you lose this other person?"

"Over a year ago," she said. "Before Debby even came to the group. Like I said, totally unrelated."

"But she was killed. Just like Debby."

Naomi gave the slightest of nods.

"I'm sorry I don't know too much about this line of work you are in, but is it normal for attackers to return to the same victim?"

She shook her head and gripped the steering wheel tighter with both hands. She felt her palms grow damp and slip a bit on the wheel. Sawyer's words were her worst nightmare. "I—I asked Cassie the same question at your store. Typically, it's only if they know their attacker." She took solace in the fact that she didn't know hers and had no reason to ever cross paths with him again.

Suddenly, a vehicle fell into place behind them and rammed their fender. The powerful blast echoed off the cliffs and the car jolted into a spin.

Naomi let out a scream as she tried to regain control of the car.

"Hang on!" Sawyer yelled and reached to help her with the wheel as the car spun around. He felt it rise on one side, right before it flipped upside down. The windows smashed in and the roof crumpled down on them. The car continued to roll in a deafening sound of crunching metal and breaking glass before it came to rest upside down.

The eerie sound of silence filled the aftermath as Sawyer hung upside down, still connected to the seat by his seat belt. His head felt like a heavy weight as he attempted to turn it to see Naomi. He could barely move it but managed to see her out of the corner of his eye.

She was also upside down, but not moving.

"Naomi," he whispered harshly. Clearing his throat, he tried again, louder. At no response, panic set in. His breathing picked up as his mind registered the possibility of her being dead. "No, no, no, no! Naomi, answer me!" He reached for his seat belt buckle, fumbling for it until he made contact.

One click, and his whole body fell to the crunched and broken roof of the car. He bent his head forward, so his back took the brunt of the impact and pain. He groaned loudly but bit back the discomfort as he tried to get to Naomi.

A sound from outside stopped his movement. He listened intently and realized it was a person. Someone was out there.

"Help!" Sawyer yelled. "Please, help us!"

But when he looked up from his upside-down position, he saw the tip of a handgun outside the driver's window. It pointed down beside a pair of men's business pants. Sawyer couldn't see above the knees of the man, only his lower legs and the gun.

Then the gun rose and the sound of it locking told him what was to come. The gun was cocked and Naomi's head was right in the line of fire.

Sawyer had no way to stop her from being hit. From his position all he could do was reach up for her seat belt buckle.

In the next second, the gunman said, "All you had to do was keep your mouth shut." He pointed the barrel into the car just as bright headlights appeared around the cliff and a tractor trailer blew its horn into the dark night.

Sawyer pushed Naomi's belt button, and she fell in a thud into Sawyer's waiting arms, while the gun blasted around them.

Sawyer pulled her with all his might toward his side. "Please, *Gott*, help me," he cried out as he struggled to know how to protect this woman. This woman who was always a part of him. As children, as teenagers and now as adults. She would always be a part of him. No matter where she lived.

The truck came to a stop beside the car, and a door slammed. "Hey!" a man yelled. "Is anyone in there?"

"Ya!" Sawyer yelled. "There's a shooter! Watch out!"

The trucker bent down on Sawyer's side to peer in. "There's no one here now. I already radioed for an ambulance. Help is on the way."

"Can you pull her out? She's unconscious," Sawyer said, hoping his words were the truth, and she wasn't dead in his arms. "Are you sure the gunman isn't out there still?"

The man looked around. "He's gone. I think I scared him when I came around the bend with my lights blaring right on him. I didn't get a good look. Just know he was wearing a round-brimmed hat."

"And business pants," Sawyer said as the man lifted Naomi up under the arms and pulled her out through the broken window. "That's all I saw of him."

"Whoa," the truck driver said as he knelt beside Naomi's lifeless body. "You're Amish?"

"Ya, and we're under attack." He attempted to climb out but couldn't. The man came over and reached in to pull him out like he had Naomi. Once Sawyer was free from the mangled car, he knelt beside Naomi and tried to locate a pulse. "I don't know what I'm looking for," he said in frustration when he couldn't find a heartbeat.

Or maybe there wasn't one to find.

Sawyer bit back the tears closing his throat. He wouldn't accept it and leaned down to hear if she was breathing. "Come on, *liebe*. Stay with me, love."

Sirens drifted to them on the night breeze. Still so far off.

The man knelt down on the other side of Naomi and felt for a pulse. After a few silent moments, he nodded encouragingly and said, "I think I found it. It's faint, but it's there." He leaned down and confirmed she was breathing too. "She's alive. For now."

Sawyer reached to remove her *kapp* and realized it was soaked. Pulling it away and lifting it in the truck's headlights, he saw the blood. "It's her head." He immediately searched for the wound. "She's got a gash on the top of her head. It might have been the bullet. I might not have gotten her down in time."

"We'll let the paramedics decide." He looked beyond Sawyer. "They're coming up now. Let's let them do their work." He tapped Sawyer on the shoulder to move back as the ambulance screeched up beside them. "Come on," he said again when Sawyer couldn't relinquish his hold of her just yet. The man tugged him harder, and Sawyer had to lift his hands off her and move away.

Discussions and protocol on moving her blurred together as Sawyer stood off to the side and watched them handle Naomi with care. When they lifted her into the ambulance, she still hadn't regained consciousness. The doors closed, blocking his view of her from then on.

"Sir, I'd like to examine you to be sure you aren't also suffering from an injury."

"I'm fine," he said, but he did allow the paramedic to sit him down and take his vitals. "She took the worst of it all. I shouldn't have agreed to this."

"No, you shouldn't have." Sheriff Shaw appeared

behind the first responder. "She was supposed to be kept hidden. What happened?"

"I'm so sorry. She was going to come to you with or without me."

"She was coming to me? Why?"

Sawyer rushed to find the folded piece of paper in his pocket. Taking it out, he passed it over to her. "Irving Adams was Debby's rapist. Naomi is certain sure of it. Find him, and you'll find the man who did this tonight. He shot at the car, then at her." His stomach roiled, and he covered his mouth.

She reached for her radio at her shoulder. "You might have a concussion. I'll get on finding this Adams guy and you let the paramedics finish checking you out. I'll be right back. Be thinking of anything you might remember."

Cassie turned away to share the information on the sheet of paper while the paramedic shone a light into his eyes.

"If there's a concussion, I think it's slight," the man confirmed and shut off his light once he was done.

Cassie returned. "Okay, you ready?" She didn't wait for a reply. "Whose car is this, and how did you get it? Last I knew Amish didn't drive."

"It's Jim Clark's, my website tech and partner. He came by and I asked him to look into Irving Adams. When he came back with the information on that paper, he offered his car."

"You asked him to play cop?" she said with pursed lips. "I was already searching for Adams. Leave the investigating to me, please."

"I wasn't sure it was anything. He was at the barn

working, and I mentioned the name. I just wanted an address, but Jim brought back all that personal information. He did that on his own."

She sighed. "Fine, whatever. Let's get back to this crime scene. The truck driver says the man had a round hat. That could fit the first shooter with a cowboy hat. Maybe the truck driver was too far to see for sure. But you were up close and personal. Did you happen to see the kind of gun he had?"

Sawyer huffed. "I saw that up close. Pointed right into the car at Naomi. It was a handgun."

"Ok, so that's the .45 shooter. Did he say anything?"

"No." Sawyer thought on that. "Wait. Maybe."

"Maybe? Can you elaborate?"

Sawyer stood up and walked around the car. He fisted his hands, trying to remember the words the man said before he fired the gun. "He definitely said something." Sawyer stood at the back of the car, trying to imagine the scene playing out again. "He aimed the gun and said something like… 'All you had to do was keep your mouth shut.'"

"'All you had to do was keep your mouth shut,'" Cassie confirmed and jotted it down on her pad.

As Sawyer turned to go back, he looked at the license plate number again. He had taken notice of it the other day and how close the numbers were to the car that had nearly run him over the night Naomi was shot.

8-3-8-3-1-7.

In the dark moment at the house, he had thought he read *B-3-8-3-1-2*. But could he have misread the *8* for a *B* and the *7* for a *2*?

Now that the car was upside down, the *7* did resemble

a flipped *2* at a quick glance. When he had read the plate at the house, he had been jumping through the air to avoid being hit. In his nearly upside-down angle, it was possible to have confused the numbers. But what about the *B*? He had thought it began with a *B*, but this plate began with an *8*. Had he read that symbol incorrectly too?

"Is something wrong?" Cassie asked. "Are you remembering anything else from the shooter?"

"Not this one, but maybe the other one. I had told you the license plate number of the car that he drove. *B-3-8-3-1-2*. Right?"

"There wasn't a match," she informed him.

He nodded at the car. "Maybe because I misread it," he explained.

"Having four numbers that do match is suspect enough for me. I'll get a warrant for Mr. Clark's house. We've got a gun to find." She moved to make the call, while Sawyer's heart ached at what this meant. Could his friend really have shot Naomi? And nearly run him over?

A few moments later, Cassie hung up the phone and announced, "Irving Adams is innocent."

"What? Are you sure?"

"At least in regard to tonight's shooting. The Louisville authorities will have to look into Debby's first attack as well as her murder. But as for tonight, Adams was tracked down with his family in Cincinnati, Ohio. He's been there all day with them at the zoo. He was nowhere near Rogues Ridge tonight. So that means we still don't have IDs on either of these shooters."

"And they're both still out there," Sawyer finished

for her. "Naomi! We just sent her in an ambulance with no guard."

"I'm on it." Cassie said, running to her cruiser. Sawyer stayed right on her heels.

THIRTEEN

Pain throbbed through Naomi's head before she even opened her eyes. She groaned with them sealed shut as she heard people talking around her. "Move her into stall 3," someone said, and before she knew it, she felt herself gliding forward.

Now she forced her eyes wide against the blaring light above. The ceiling tiles whisked by as someone behind her pushed her forward. Pushed her toward stall 3, wherever that was.

"Where am I?" she asked.

"In the hospital," the person behind her informed her.

"Again?" she asked.

"You've been here before?"

"Mmm-hmm," she answered and shut her eyes again. Just for a moment until the pain subsided.

"I'm going to leave you here. The doctor will be in shortly."

"Wait." She moved her hand to try to stop the person. "What happened? Where's Chloe? Is she all right?"

"You were in a car accident. No one else came with you. I don't know who Chloe is. Can I call her for you?"

"No, she's a baby." Naomi tried to remember what happened. She was being chased, wasn't she? No, that was a long time ago. "I was with Sawyer... Sawyer!" She pushed up on her elbows. Eye-blinding pain filled her head.

"Ma'am, lie back down," the man said, touching her shoulder.

"Where is Sawyer? Did he come in? He was with me in the car."

"Like I said, no one came in with you."

The curtain fluttered and was pushed aside. A doctor stood at the bottom of her bed and lifted a chart. "Says here you regained consciousness in the ambulance. Good, good. You do have a bad gash on the top of your head that might need stiches. Let's take a look." He stepped up beside her and felt around the top of her head. Naomi whimpered. "I know, I know. It hurts. We can get you some pain meds for that."

"No, I just want to know where Sawyer is. Did he come in?"

"As far as I know, you were brought in alone. I can make a call to the sheriff's office to find out for you. Right after I examine you." He left no room for negotiating and Naomi endured his prodding for a little while longer. "I don't feel any skull fractures, but you will have a big contusion for a few days. A few stiches should seal you up good too. I think you'll be out of here by morning. You're one of my easiest patients tonight. Good thing you were wearing your seat belt."

He grabbed the clipboard again and wrote some

information down on it. He hung it back on the bottom of the bed.

"Are you going to call about Sawyer? His name is Sawyer Zook."

"I'll look into it right now. Give me a few minutes, and I'll be right back."

Naomi closed her eyes again as the men left her. The pain was too intense to keep them open and all she wanted to do was sleep. When she felt her bed moving again, she jolted awake, realizing she had fallen asleep again.

"Sawyer?" she called out. "Is he all right? Where am I going?"

No response came from the person pushing her from behind.

"Am I being discharged?" A set of doors neared in front of her. "Hello?" The end of her bed hit the doors and pushed them wide, her speed picking up once she went through. Something didn't feel right. She suddenly didn't feel safe. "Please, stop," she said and when the bed sped up more, she tried to sit up. She took the next corner so fast, the bed tipped on its side.

Naomi screamed and grabbed the sheet beneath her with both hands. She felt it slipping from the mattress and held on to the frame. The bed straightened out, and she craned her neck to see behind her.

"Stop right there! Police!" A voice from behind shouted down the corridor. Before Naomi could twist around further, the bed tilted again, but this time, there was no holding on.

It crashed down on its side, Naomi hitting the tile hard. She let out a shout on impact as the pain jostled throughout her body and head. She tried to push herself up on one arm and caught sight of the back of the man who had been pushing her. He wore a hospital gown over his clothes, so all she saw was a pair of tan dress pants and brown leather shoes. He had a surgical cap over dark brown hair, but with his back to her as he ran to the stairwell, she couldn't see his face.

Sheriff Shaw chased after him at full speed, then suddenly, Sawyer came into view and he was all she wanted to see.

"You're alive!" she cried out, reaching for him.

He fell to his knees and scooped her up to cradle her in his lap. "So are you." He smiled brightly and held her face. He leaned down and kissed her cheek quickly. Then the other. His lips found hers next, and his quick kisses paused there. He lifted his head and suddenly looked nervous. Then he grew serious and scanned her head and down her body. "Are you hurt?"

"A gash on my head that needs to be closed, but the doctor says I can leave in the morning. That man was taking me somewhere, but I don't know where. I'm so glad you and Cassie showed up when you did."

"Do you know who it was? Was it someone you know?"

"I only saw his legs."

"Let me guess, business pants."

"*Ya*, tan."

"He's for certain sure the man who shot at you in the car."

"A man shot at me in the car?"

Sawyer pulled her close to him and hugged her tight. "I'm so glad he missed, but how much more can we face? We have to figure out who these men are and why they are after you. Are they connected to both of the women from your support group's deaths?"

Naomi stiffened in his arms. Slowly, he leaned back to search her face. "The only person who is responsible for Brie's death is me," she said. "I caused her to run out of the clinic that day. She ran out into the road, and a car hit her and took off. By the time I caught up to her, the car was gone, and she was dead. It was my fault that she ran out. I couldn't help her."

Sawyer pressed his lips. "The police need to know these details just in case Brie's death is related. But first they need to find these two gunmen who are after you. I'm sad to say my friend Jim might be one of them."

Naomi pushed up quickly. "Jim? Jim wouldn't try to kill me."

"How do you know?"

She averted her gaze from Sawyer's inquiring eyes. To share that answer would mean sharing about the night Jim helped her escape Rogues Ridge. "I just know." Her lame answer spoke volumes. The loudest message being she still didn't trust Sawyer.

A sad expression covered his face. Eyes full of disappointment, he looked to the doors. Then he stood and helped her to her feet. "We should get back in the emergency room so the doctor can help you. Hopefully, Cassie will catch this guy and figure out why he thinks you need to stop talking. I can't imagine what he thinks you need to be kept quiet about. You're the most tight-lipped person I know."

"I'm sorry to say he got away," Cassie said as she entered Naomi's cubicle an hour later. Naomi was just finished being stitched up but was still hooked to the IV. Cassie continued in her authoritative demeanor to relay the current status. "He obviously had a car ready and waiting where he planned to take you. He was gone before I got down the stairs and outside." She dropped into the chair beside the bed, her face full of remorse. "Did you get a good look at him?"

Sawyer glanced Naomi's way and at her frown, he said, "I could be all wrong about this, but there may be a connection to the support group."

Cassie straightened up in her chair. "Please, enlighten me."

Sawyer explained what he heard the man say before he pulled the trigger. "There have been two suspicious deaths in Naomi's support group. Maybe they are connected to her because of something she said in the group. Something she was supposed to keep quiet about."

"How did the other woman die again?" Cassie asked Naomi.

"She was hit by a car, but I don't see the connection. Brie was crossing the street leaving the support group. She had been very upset and crying when she ran out. I went after her, but when I got there, a crowd was already surrounding her. She was dead on impact. It has nothing to do with me."

"And the driver?" Cassie asked.

"Never found. It was a hit-and-run. She died before she ever found healing and ran out believing her attacker would never let her go. Maybe he didn't. I've had my suspicions that he found her that day."

Cassie sighed and leaned her head back against the wall. Her eyes closed in what seemed to be true despair and disappointment. Sawyer saw an officer of the law caring about people she didn't even know. He looked to Naomi's crestfallen face and realized she was also in a profession that expected the same.

Expected? Or did Naomi go above and beyond her duty?

And why?

"The people who come into your lives come with little to no hope," Sawyer said to them both. "The Amish way of charity is our way of life, but we still separate ourselves from the world and its problems to protect our lives. How do you do your jobs of public service and still protect yours?"

Cassie lifted her head and tilted it at the question. "I suppose it's something we are called to do, and that's part of the deal. We know going in it won't be easy. And it will be dangerous." She looked to Naomi and shrugged. "But to help someone, even just one, feels like we're doing God's work, wouldn't you say, Naomi?"

Naomi frowned but nodded. "I confess I cut Him out of my work, but I know what you mean. I care so much for each woman who walks through my door. We share our stories in the most confidential manner. We trust each other that no word goes beyond that room, and because of that we bond in the most unguarded way. I train them to be stronger and give them all the tools to protect themselves, both mentally and physically. I care about each one of them and help them get their life back."

As Sawyer listened, he became more convinced Naomi suffered something horrible. "Our?" he asked.

"Pardon?" Naomi said.

"You said, 'we share *our* stories.' What did you mean?"

A red hue spread up from Naomi's neck. He could see she struggled with a response. Her flitted glance toward Cassie told him the sheriff had been privy to Naomi's past, but he was not.

"Do you not see that what you give to these women is what you withhold from yourself? Don't you also want your life back?"

"More than anything," Naomi whispered with downcast eyes. "But if everyone knew the truth, it would not be the life I wanted."

"Or people would see how strong you are. Don't you think that would really help these women get their lives back? To see you get back up and retake what someone stole from you?"

Tears filled her eyes. "You don't know what you're asking. Tell him, Cassie. Tell him how there are bad people out there who thrive on hurting people. Not everyone gets to stand back up again. Some lives are ruined forever."

"Only Brie's and Debby's," Sawyer said. "They won't get another chance at reclaiming their lives. But you can."

Cassie stood up. "The two of you need to have a talk. Sawyer, be gentle. And, Naomi, open your eyes to what he is offering you. It's a risk, I know, but remember the only people who matter are the ones who believe in you. I need to step out and make a call. I'll be back in a little while."

"Wait!" Naomi sat up straight. Her face drained of color.

Sawyer jumped to his feet, ready to hit the call button. "Is something wrong? You match your white sheet."

Naomi pushed the sheet off her and moved to sit on the edge of the bed. When she reached for the IV in her arm, he grabbed her hand to stop her.

"The women! I have to get out of here," she cried. "There are five other women in the group. If it's true that someone's targeting the whole group, then the others are not safe. I have to warn them."

Cassie passed over a pad and pen. "Write their names and contact info. I will take care of contacting them and getting their local PDs to protect them. That's my job. I'll also have an unmarked car bring you back to the farm. Then have him stake out there from now on. No more taking chances, got it?"

Naomi shook her head. "That's impossible."

"Your safety is all that matters. You need to stay there."

"No, I mean I can't share the women's information. It's confidential. It puts them at risk."

"I think it's too late for that, Naomi," Sawyer cut in and hunched low in front of her to meet her at eye level. Taking her hands into his, he drew her attention and implored her to listen to him. To trust him this time and what he had to say. For her own safety. "You have to let the police protect them now. Don't you see? If some-one is after them, he already has the names." Sawyer shook her hands when she looked over his shoulder. "He has the list already, Naomi. And you're on it too.

Let Cassie do what she does best. Protect people. Give her the names."

He saw the debate in her eyes. But when they darkened, he knew his words were not penetrating her resolve to protect these women's names and stories. He knew she would take them to her grave. Even if that grave was just around the corner.

"I admire your loyalty," he said. "Those women are blessed to have you in their lives. You are a true friend to them, but I have to believe they would want to know if someone was coming after them. I know they will forgive you for breaking confidence in this instance."

"You don't understand. Everyone will know the truth," she whispered, and her hands trembled in his. She visibly shook, as if her temperature plummeted in a second.

Sawyer peered out the corner of his eye at Cassie. Her expression wasn't the sympathetic officer he expected to see. Instead, she raised her eyebrows at him as though she was waiting for him to come clean.

But he hadn't done anything wrong.

Had he?

It appeared he had his own decision to make.

"I'll leave you two alone, so you can…talk. I think you have some things to rectify. Don't be long. Lives are at stake." Cassie swept the curtain closed after she exited, but the lack of her footsteps told him she didn't go far.

"What does she mean by 'things to rectify'?" Naomi asked. Her timid voice reminded him of her eighteen-year-old self.

"She means... She means I have a lot to apologize for. I'm sorry."

"For what?" She eyed him cautiously.

Everything was so clear now. He could see all the times he had the opportunity to be just as loyal to her as she was to the women in her support group.

"I should have gone after you," he whispered as the guilt swamped him. "If I could go back, I would do it differently. I would tell everyone they were wrong. That you weren't the wild child they thought you were. I should have vouched for you. I shouldn't have accepted your leaving and searched for you. I would have been the man worthy of you. I would have stood alone if I had to. Because the truth is worth it. How can I expect you to tell me the truth if I've never earned the right to know?"

Tears pooled in her eyes, and for the first time since she returned he could see her pain of bearing this trauma all alone.

He did this. He did this to her.

"How different your life might have been if I had stood by you and believed in you. If I searched for you and went after you."

Naomi's mouth opened to the sound of the most heart-wrenching anguish he had ever heard. He reached for her and wrapped her tightly up in his arms, lifting her from the bed and supporting her trembling body. Her cries pressed deep into his neck. It was what should have happened eight years ago, but now it wouldn't fix anything. The damage was already done. Their trust was forever broken, because when she needed him most, he wasn't there.

"James Clark knew," she whispered against him when her wails had subsided.

Sawyer sputtered at this information. "Jim? *My* Jim?"

She sniffed and nodded against him. "I always prayed he would break his word to me and tell you I'd been attacked. That I didn't leave the Amish on my own. So you would come and get me. He knew where I was. He brought me there. He found me by the dumpster and brought me to Edna's boarding house."

Sawyer's mind couldn't comprehend any of these details. He remembered Jim's remark in the barn about keeping her secret. *This was the secret?* That he had whisked an abused Amish girl off into the night? *Why?* It was unfathomable that the man came to work every day for all these years, sat beside him and never thought he might want to know.

Anger like Sawyer had never known stirred within him. His Amish ways would be tested with this one. Jim had even tried to convince him to marry, when Sawyer had avoided the very idea for three years. *Why would he do that?*

"He never said a word," he mumbled his thoughts aloud and felt his head flare with an unfamiliar rage. "All this time…and he was the one who took you away from me?" Sawyer stepped back and grabbed at his head. "How could he?"

"Don't be mad at him. I asked him not to tell. I couldn't face you. Not after what happened in that house. You had told me not to go to the party. You had warned Liza and me, but I went anyway. I just wanted to run away and never look back."

Sawyer froze with his hands in his hair. Slowly, he brought them down as a sickening feeling rolled through him. "Naomi, I have to know. Is Jim the one who hurt you?"

Her gaze fell in an instant to her clenched hands in front of her. She shook her head. "But I don't know who did… I don't know who he is. I have a first name, but I don't even know if it's real. I had been knocked unconscious and my memory is skewed. Jim's the one who found me outside by the dumpster."

Sawyer closed his eyes at the horrid image she portrayed. How could anyone treat another human being with such disrespect? It was beyond him. He let out a deep breath and pulled in more slow and steady breaths. He pushed the image aside for another time. Right now Naomi's safety was all that mattered. That and the safety of the women at risk.

"I'm sorry if I shared too much," she said.

"Excuse me? Why would you apologize for that?"

"I know the details make people uncomfortable. I can't fault them. It's nothing anyone wants to imagine, and it's nothing they can. Nor should. It's why we have support groups. It's a place we can share freely and safely with those who understand. We trust each other with our deepest fears and even the details. That's why our meetings are confidential. Sometimes we share things like names and places that we don't want getting out."

"You tell me whatever you need to, and I will keep things between us. I promise. You've carried it alone for far too long. I wish you had told someone here. Anyone. Even if not me."

"I told Jim. He helped me get to Edna's after we stopped at a motel to get cleaned up. He helped me. The best he could, I guess."

"Helped you," Sawyer repeated her words that made no sense to him. "Did you ever question his reasons?"

"Not until I went to school to train to be a counselor. I learned the correct protocol and realized I did everything wrong that night."

"No, Jim did everything wrong that night. Jim should have brought you right to the hospital. Jim didn't help you. Letting more harm come to someone isn't helping them. And that's exactly what he did. He sent you out into the world, an Amish girl with no English world experience, to fend for yourself. And didn't tell anyone. You tell me not to be mad, but I'm struggling to understand such cruelty."

Sawyer thought of the license plate being so close to what he saw the night of the shooting on his sister's farm. Before, he wouldn't have believed his friend was involved in something so evil, but in this light, that thought wavered to a great possibility. *But why?*

"It was eight years ago," Naomi said. "It doesn't matter anymore. I thrived. I moved on. We all did."

Sawyer scoffed. "Not everyone. Don't forget you took a bullet in your side from someone who hasn't moved on." *But why would Jim shoot her?*

"If the deaths are related to the support group, then the shooter has nothing to do with my assault."

"There have been two separate guns used. You could have two people trying to kill you for two separate reasons." His eyes bored into hers as he pleaded, "Tell Cassie the women's names so the police can keep them safe until they find the attackers. That would be really helping these women."

Naomi looked to the pad of paper sitting on the bed where Cassie had left it. After only a moment's hesitation, she reached for it and flipped it open to begin writing.

A minute later she closed it and pushed it back to him. "I hope I don't live to regret this."

He nodded. "At least you'll be alive."

He hoped.

FOURTEEN

Little Ben was the only person to say one word to Naomi since her return to Anna's house.

It's clear I have officially worn out my welcome, Naomi thought as she cleared the table after dinner two days later and started to bring the dishes to the pump and basin to wash them. Before she reached the sink, Anna stepped in her way and took the stack from her. She said no words, but she made it clear she didn't want the help.

Naomi was excused.

She turned to the living room, where people were chatting and playing, oblivious to the tension going on between the woman of the house and the unwanted guest. Her gaze fell on Sawyer bouncing Chloe on his knees. She did her best to let his joy and excitement with the baby ease her distress. He never looked happier than in this moment.

He will make a good daed *someday.*

The idea only made her sadder. She checked her emotions quickly, not wanting the direction of her thoughts conveyed to all. But for Sawyer to be a father, it would mean he found a wife.

The idea caught her breath, and she felt her plastered smile waver. She averted her gaze to regain control and stared out the kitchen window into the dark night. Somewhere out there, one of Cassie's deputies guarded the home, offering her some semblance of peace, but that didn't include peace in Anna's home.

Naomi took a deep breath and rejoined the group. As she turned to face them all, she caught Sawyer staring at her with concern on his face. He stood and secured the baby against his side. His walk toward her made her light-headed the closer he came.

"What's wrong?" he whispered.

Naomi shook her head and kept her smile on to the point her cheeks ached.

Suddenly, he thrust Chloe into her arms as he looked at his sister's back in the kitchen. "This ends right now," he said and bypassed her before she could stop him.

"No, Sawyer, wait," Naomi whispered harshly, as not to bring more attention to them. But her words fell on deaf ears. Sawyer continued for his sister.

The next minutes that followed were more horrifying than anything Naomi could have imagined. For eight years, she wondered what might have been if she had stayed in Rogues Ridge.

Now she knew.

"I won't let you treat Naomi so poorly anymore," Sawyer said loud and clear for all to hear.

"And I won't let Naomi put you in harm's way any

longer," Anna responded straight in her brother's face. She threw down the hand towel on the counter and started to untie her apron in quick, jerky movements.

Naomi held Chloe closer as the baby started to whimper at the tension escalating in the house. She controlled her own whimpering that threatened to slip out.

"Please, stop," she said to both.

Anna flashed angry eyes at her. "This is my home. I extended charity to you, and you repay me by putting my *brudder* in all this danger. There is a reason the Amish do not mingle with the English. You brought that dark world into my home, and I will never forget that. You don't belong here anymore. You made your choice when you left."

"Enough!" Sawyer yelled.

Instant nausea burst up in Naomi's stomach. She stepped back as if Anna had hit her with her fists, bending her in half and nearly breaking her in two with her sharp words of judgment.

Chloe let out a screeching cry of fear in the heated atmosphere.

"You don't know what you are saying, Anna," Sawyer said, his voice barely under control. "You don't know the truth."

"Stop, Sawyer," Naomi cried out, even more abhorred about what he was about to do. She felt the walls closing in on her. She had to get out of there. A searing panic shook her and blocked her mind from thinking clearly.

"Nothing will change if she doesn't know the truth," he pleaded with her.

"You shouldn't have to know everyone's truth to treat them kindly. You should treat them kindly despite not knowing." Naomi turned and found all eyes on her. Even little Ben's lip quivered in fear. "I'm sorry I came here. I thought it would be safe. But I'm in more danger with people who never believed in me than I ever would be with strangers."

She made a direct line for the back door. She swung it wide and ran out into the night without a clear thought of what she was doing or where she was going.

"Naomi!" Sawyer shouted from behind. His footsteps hit the steps at a fast clip, but she was already in the driveway. The road beckoned ahead.

Cassie had said she put an officer on the street, but with no streetlights it could be parked anywhere. She tucked Chloe's head down to keep her from being jostled and pushed toward the end of the driveway.

She prayed the officer would see her and ride up to pick her up. The faster she got out of here, the better it would be for all.

The better it would be for Sawyer.

She knew he meant well by standing up for her with his sister, but more strife didn't help anyone. There was a reason the Amish didn't mingle with outsiders. It threatened chaos to the order of things. It broke up family units.

Sawyer's thudding feet were right behind her now. The street met the end of the driveway just as his hand grabbed hold of her shoulder.

"Don't go, Naomi," he said, and she could tell tears choked his throat. Fear threaded his voice, and for a moment she questioned her decision to leave.

"It's for the best," she said, trying to convince them both. "You've lost so much. I won't let you lose your family too."

Naomi turned away and spotted the headlights of a vehicle coming their way. She sighed in relief at being spotted by the officer. She'd find another place to hide until Cassie tracked down this gunman, or men, or whatever.

"I've lost so much?" He pulled her back to look at him. "It started with losing you. I loved you, and you broke my heart."

The pain in his voice threatened to crush her resolve. "I was scared. I'm sorry my leaving hurt you, Sawyer. I couldn't face you. I couldn't face anyone. But you moved on. And you will again. You'll have your family."

"I want *you*! Don't you understand?" He stepped in front of her to block her way to the road. "It's always been you." He stilled, his face inches from hers and eyes begging her to do what she couldn't. "Come back to me, Naomi," he whispered. "Stay. Stay forever."

It all sounded so perfect. How many times had she dreamed he would come for her with his arms outstretched? Now here he was repeating the words of her dreams.

Dreams. Not reality.

"I'm not Amish anymore," she said. "And I can't be."

She closed her eyes. The sound of the engine rumbled closer at a slow pace. She expected it to be the officer on guard duty, but a truck stopped right behind her. She searched the dark roads for the deputy's vehicle. He was supposed to be close by.

"Is everything all right?" A male voice spoke out the window.

Before Naomi could figure who was behind the wheel, Sawyer glanced over his shoulder, and his lips contorted into a sneer. "Jim Clark. How convenient for you to show up."

"Hey, Sawyer, I was just passing by on my way home. It looked like you could use some help. I know things have been dangerous for you both lately. I heard about my car. But don't worry. I'm just glad to know the two of you are safe."

"Thank you, but we won't be needing your help," Sawyer said. "That goes for the business too."

"Whoa, did I miss something?" Jim asked.

"I know what you did. How you took Naomi from here. From *me*. And you let me believe the worst about what happened that night."

Naomi touched his shirt with her free arm. "Don't do this, Sawyer."

"He took you from me."

"No. He saved you from having to be associated with me. You would not have been able to stand by me then. And you won't be able to now."

"How do you know? You've never given me a chance to try."

Naomi shrank back at his accusation. Except, it was the truth. She'd made all the decisions for him since that night. He'd asked her not to go to the party, and even then, she'd disregarded his opinion.

"You're right," she said simply. "I always thought I was saving you from pain by leaving, but I see now I only caused you more. I don't want to do that to you again, but I can't go back in that house, Sawyer. I don't deserve that treatment either. What do you want me to do? Tell me, and this time, I promise to listen. But please don't make me go back in there."

The crushed expression on his face showed how this situation with his sister also hurt him.

"I don't want to make you choose." Naomi lifted up on her feet and touched his cheek with her lips. Tears filled her eyes at the contact of his stubbly face against her. So real. She breathed deep. So final.

"Don't go," he said quickly and grabbed hold of her back and pulled her and Chloe into his embrace. "We'll go to the officer and have him bring us somewhere safe. We'll go together. Tonight. Right now."

"Are you sure?" she whispered.

He dropped his forehead to hers and smiled. "I've never been surer of anything in my life."

From the truck, Jim cleared his throat. "Is everything all right?"

Without turning her head, Naomi said, "I don't need your help, Jim. I never did."

"Suit yourself." The squeal of his truck's tires against the pavement jerked her shoulders, but not as much as her laughter that followed. "That felt good," she said once they were alone. "I wish I had said that eight years ago."

"Me too." Sawyer's somber voice vibrated against her forehead. He placed his lips against her forehead and kissed her sweetly there. Then he took Chloe from her arms. With the baby cradled in the crook of his arm, he took her hand and led her down the street.

They walked quietly toward an unknown world he

knew nothing of, and one she wasn't excited about returning to. But they would do this together.

The front of the deputy's cruiser glinted in the moonlight from behind a hedge of bushes. Naomi expected the officer to come out to meet them, but with each step closer, the stillness of the scene slowed her steps.

"Something's wrong," she said.

"*Ya*, I sense it too. Stay here." He waved for her to stop as he moved closer to the car. "Officer?" he called. "Is everything all right?"

Naomi couldn't see inside the car, only Sawyer bending over to look inside.

"Naomi, get back to the house!" He straightened up and turned back with Chloe in a run toward her.

"What happened?" she asked.

"He's been shot. Now, run!"

Naomi froze in place. Her feet felt weighted down at Sawyer's words. She couldn't move. "H-how?"

In the next moment, the squeal of tires resounded down the road. A turn of her head showed Jim's truck was coming back. Naomi forced her feet to move slowly toward the road, then faster as he neared. They needed his help now.

"Naomi, no!" Sawyer yelled, but now she was running.

The truck slowed quickly, but before it stopped, the passenger-side door opened, and a man jumped out.

It wasn't Jim.

Before she could back away, the man had her in his arms and lifted her off the ground. He threw her inside, jumped in behind her and the truck took off before the door was shut. With her face pressed against the seat,

Naomi struggled to breathe. As they pulled farther away from Sawyer, she knew this time he would come for her. But would he find her in time?

FIFTEEN

The truck came to an abrupt stop, but, wedged down between the seats, Naomi was unable to see where she was and who had her. The whole ride couldn't have been more than fifteen minutes, and when she heard the driver's-side door open and slam shut, she screamed, "Help me! Help me!"

She hoped someone nearby would hear her pleas and call the police.

The kidnapper laughed. "Yell all you want. No one will hear you this far from town." Then he pulled her hands tight behind her and bound them. A bag came over her head next, and she writhed in response. He yanked her off the floor and dragged her out the passenger door, standing her on her feet.

"Walk," he said.

"I can't see where I'm going."

He pushed her from behind, sending her forward. She stumbled and fell to her knees with no way to catch her fall. Pain radiated up her legs, but in the next second the man pulled her up by her hair, and she cried out from his rough treatment of her.

"Why are you doing this?" she asked, taking a blind step forward, testing the ground with careful footing as she felt his hand press into her back.

"I'm finishing what I started before you ruined everything with your big mouth," he snarled and picked her up. "You're too slow. I'll just have to carry you inside."

"Inside? Where are we?" Her voice squeaked as he jostled her.

"Hold the door," the man said, and she realized the driver must still be around and was helping this man kidnap her.

"Please, help me," she called out, but the other person didn't respond. "Jim? Is it you? You've helped me before. You helped me escape."

The man holding her tightened his hold. "That was his first mistake. It won't happen again."

"Jim? It is you," she said, hope threading her voice. The man holding her might as well have confirmed it with his words. "You can stop this."

"Not stop, but finish. What started eight years ago is going to be finished tonight," her unknown kidnapper said. "You couldn't just go away like a good little Amish girl. You had to open your mouth. Now I have to make sure it's shut for good." The sound of shoes scuffled along wood floor as her body was held tight against a hard chest and moved to unknown places. The man's voice echoed as though the place was empty of furniture. She heard the sound of a match and saw a glow of light seep through the cloth bag over her head.

A lantern.

So they were somewhere with no electricity.

She sniffed through the cloth and smelled the mildew of a damp place. Some vacant building, maybe? Somewhere where no one would hear her scream. She had no hope of being found or noticed by a stranger. Jim was her only hope.

Naomi jammed her feet back to kick the man's shins. He grunted but his hold stayed strong.

"Nice try, but that's why I tied your hands. Jim told me how you fought back the night in the barn and got away. I'm not taking any chances." The man's heavy shoes clunked up wooden stairs.

Were they in a house?

Naomi put aside her questions for what her captor had just said. Jim told him about how she fought and broke free the night in the barn.

Jim told me.

"Jim? You tried to kill me that night? You threw the saw blade at my head? I trusted you. I told Sawyer you wouldn't hurt me."

"And I told you never to tell anyone about the night here." Jim's voice came from above. He stood at the top of the staircase that she was being carried up.

"The night here?" Her voice squeaked. *It couldn't be.* "You brought me back to that place?"

Jim spoke low. "We're back to where it all happened. I gave you a chance to move on and forget about this place, but you chose to talk about it in your women's group. Did you ever think one of them might spread the word?"

"Of course not," Naomi said, trying to shake her arms free from the strong man grasping her. "Everything spoken there is confidential."

Jim huffed. "You really are naive. Then explain to me why a woman named Brie Carlson came to Rogues Ridge and threatened to go public if she didn't get paid?"

"B-Brie came to Rogues Ridge?"

A door creaked open, and Naomi felt herself being brought into another space. *Oh, please, don't let it be the room.*

But she knew as soon as she was thrown into a chair that it was exactly where Jim and this man had brought her. "Why are you tormenting me? Why now?"

"Because of Brie. You see, Naomi, I am not really a killer. I am a protector. But when Brie Carlson showed up, demanding money to keep her from going to the press about happened in this room, you made me do things I didn't want to do. You made me kill. Not once, but twice. Now I have to make sure anyone else who knows what happened here eight years ago isn't able to come knocking again."

"You killed Brie and Debby?" The air rushed from her lungs. "It was you? I don't understand why you care that I shared in the support group. I'm sorry Brie came looking for money, but I don't understand why it matters to you."

In the next second, the cloth bag over her head was torn off to reveal Jim standing by the door with a lantern in his hand. The golden light cast three shadows on the walls. She turned her head to get a glimpse of the man who had carried her up there. With the light glowing on his face, she had a bright view and immediately recognized him from this very room eight years ago.

Naomi's breath caught in her chest and she quickly

started to hyperventilate. She jumped to her feet, but the man stepped close and pushed her hard, back in the chair.

"I see you remember my brother," Jim said.

"Your brother?" she whispered, unable to take her eyes off the man who frequented her nightmares.

Jim laughed, a sick twist in his voice. "You didn't actually think I helped you leave town out of the kindness of my heart, did you?"

Naomi thought of Sawyer's opinion of Jim. Jim hadn't been helping her. He had been helping himself. Or, more accurately, his *brother*.

"You knew who did it all along?" She shook her head back and forth as short, uneven breaths escaped her lips. Flashes of that night in this room chilled her mind from forming a plan. All she could do was stare at this man's face. "Keith." She said the only name she remembered of him.

He smiled, and if she didn't know him, she would have thought he was a good-looking and trustworthy young man. Just like she had thought eight years ago when he'd brought her to this room to chat, as he had said.

Then Naomi remembered Sawyer telling her Jim's brother was some sort of politician. Jim hadn't been helping her but helping his brother from going down for attacking a young Amish woman.

"I'll leave you two alone." Jim put down the lantern on the wood floor. "You have a lot to catch up on." He tipped an invisible hat that caused her to remember the cowboy hat he had worn the night he pushed her off the road and shot at her. "Naomi, it was nice to see you again. Sorry this will be the last time. If I were you, I'd give my brother those names. He's not as helpful as I am."

Jim stepped out of the room and closed the door behind him.

"Jim!" she called out. "Please don't leave me here with him."

"This time he won't be coming to your aid." Keith spoke quietly as he put on leather gloves. "You can make this easy on yourself by telling the names of any other people you blabbed to in or out of your group. But whether you tell me or not, I will find them."

"I never told anyone in the group your name," Naomi said. "Brie only knew about Jim because she asked me privately. I wanted her to press charges against her attacker, but she said since I never did, why should she. I told her about Jim helping me. She was living on the streets and must have thought she could get money from him. I don't know why she did that, and I wish she hadn't, but there's no reason to hurt anyone else. You have to believe me."

"Is that your answer?"

She stilled and swallowed hard, staring at his gloved hands so close to her face. She looked up to meet his gaze and nodded. "I'm not telling you anyone's names. They're confidential."

"You're making a big mistake. You can't beat me. Do you have any idea who I am now? And who I'm going to become? I'm heading to the US Senate."

Naomi curled her lip. "Funny, because all I see is some spoiled man who thinks he can get away with anything. You knew you would never pay for your crime against an unsuspecting Amish girl who just wanted to be included with the kids her age. I came here that night thinking I might make a few friends. Or at least have a little fun before I committed to the church and became baptized. Before I gave the man I loved my acceptance to his proposal. It was one night to pretend to be someone I wasn't. One night that stole my life and marriage away forever. You're nothing but a fraud and a thief, and since you need your big brother to protect you, you're not even a good one at that."

Quick as lightning, Keith backhanded Naomi so hard, she went flying off the chair and skidding across the floor. With her hands still tied behind her, she had no way of stopping herself from colliding into the lantern sitting by the door.

Her leg hit the glass-and-metal lantern, knocking it on its side. With a clatter the glass shattered, and the lantern rolled away from Naomi. At eye level with the floor, she saw the flame touch the old wood floorboards, but before she could call out the danger, Keith lifted her off the ground and shook her inches from his irate face.

"I want names. Now!"

"Never."

Keith swung her around and slammed her against the window. The impact was so hard, all her breath expelled in a rush and the glass cracked against her back. A flame burst from behind him, but no words could be formed on her lips. He shook her again against the glass. "Give me the names, or I will throw you out this window right now."

Naomi choked out, "I...won't let...you hurt any...one else."

He sneered his frustrations. He had no intentions of letting her go free this time, even if she told him. They would all surely end up dead by this maniac's hand.

"You'll never...make this...go away," she forced out even as bright stars flashed in her eyes with the loss of oxygen. "There's no way...you can kill...them all."

Her eyelids fluttered closed.

He shook her. "Start talking!" he yelled in her face. "Or have a baby's death on your hands."

Naomi opened her eyes at the mention of the child. "Chloe. What...have you done?"

"Nothing...yet."

"You leave...her alone!"

"Then start talking."

The fire spread behind him and reached to the ceiling. At her wide eyes, he turned and saw the fiery flames licking the walls and creeping closer to them. The flames were seeking oxygen from the fresh air outside. With the cracked window behind him, it wouldn't take much more to break it completely.

Instantly, Naomi lifted her knees, and with all her might, she kicked her legs straight out to make direct impact with his gut. He fell back in surprise but held on to her upper arm and neck. She took the element of surprise as her instructor had taught her and lifted her legs again. This time he let go of her neck, and she fell to the floor. He reached down to pick her up, but Naomi scrambled around him for the door. The next second, she felt him grab hold of the back of her dress's collar and pull her to a stop. But Naomi couldn't let him get a secure hold of her again.

In a quick twist, Naomi sprang right back up, and, with her head bent down, she plowed right into his stomach, pushing him back against the window.

This time the glass smashed outward with an ear-splitting sound. But his scream was even louder as he teetered in the windowless opening, his arms flailing for purchase. Before he could grasp the frame, the flames rushed the window for air.

Keith screamed louder and lifted his arms to shield his face. In trying to block the fire, his body lost its balance and with one last scream he fell out the window and down to the walkway below.

Naomi's breath seized in her lungs and for a moment she couldn't move. Then, as adrenaline raced through her veins, she fell back against the wall and looked at the growing fire at the broken window. Sharp, jagged pieces of glass were still attached to the frame, like the teeth of a saw. There were broken pieces on the floor at her feet. Bending quickly, she grabbed one that fit in her hand. Keeping her eyes averted from the body on the ground, she stood back up and rushed to the closed door as the flames encroached. The old wood floorboards cracked and splintered, burning up quickly. She had to keep moving before the floors caved in.

She ran to the door but with her hands still tied, she had to turn her back to open it. Once it was opened, the smoke and flames flowed out, scorching her back and pushing her forward. The floor beneath her creaked as it weakened from the flames. It wouldn't be long before the fire fell through to the first floor and the house was ablaze. Working the glass shard against the ropes on her hands behind her, she headed toward the stairs. At any second, she expected to see Jim. She held back to cut through the ropes. She would need her hands if she found him. She cut through with only a couple slips, and when the ropes fell off her, she was at the top of the stairs. She started to toss the glass shard away but thought better of the idea.

Jim had killed Brie and Debby, and, whether he wanted to admit it or not, that made him a killer. She didn't think twice that he would kill her too.

Every available deputy in three townships parked their cars in front of Anna's home. Plans were made, and some drove off to follow their orders. Sawyer stood with Bishop Bontrager and Esau, feeling useless to help Naomi.

"I should be out there." He waved a hand to encompass the clear night.

"She could be anywhere," Esau said. "She could already be—"

"Stop." Sawyer halted him before his brother-in-law could voice what had run through his mind multiple times already. Sawyer touched his chest over his heart. It ached, but he wasn't ready to accept Naomi's death. "She will fight."

"Fighting isn't condoned," the bishop said quietly. He had come out to be with the family when Anna asked for their community's elder to be with the family for prayer. "But I pray *Gott* provides for her safety."

Sawyer replied, "Maybe I've spent too much time

with the English, but I pray Naomi's self-defense classes come in handy while *Gott* is doing His avenging."

"I've been meaning to talk to you about the English pieces you've been building," Bishop Bontrager said. "Is there a reason for your compromising of the Amish ways?"

Sawyer contemplated his answer, but all he could come up with was Jim Clark's influence over his life. The man even had him building a gun case. "Forgive me, Bishop. All I can say is my eyes see clearly now." Sawyer looked up into the sky. "What I once thought as harmless, I now see—smoke?"

"You see smoke?" Bishop asked. "How so?"

"Look." Sawyer pointed out above the trees. "At the coal mine. Is it on fire?"

The three men started moving out to the street with their eyes glued to the hills ahead. As it become obvious that a fire burned freely, Sawyer picked up his speed and ran to Sheriff Shaw's vehicle. "There's a fire out at the mine!" he yelled as soon as he saw her bent over the hood of her car, looking at a map. He ran up to her side. "She's got to be there!"

Cassie looked to the sky, then grabbed the map off the car. She threw it to the ground and ran to her driver's-side door. She shouted orders to the nearby officers to follow her.

Sawyer ran to the passenger side and climbed in.

"What do you think you're doing?" Cassie asked.

"Fixing my mistake from earlier. This time, I'm going after her."

She pursed her lips. "Don't make me regret this."

Sawyer watched the smoke billowing above. The fire

was raging. If Naomi was in that, he would be going in, and there was nothing Cassie could do to stop him. "Sorry, Sheriff, I won't guarantee anything."

"How did I know you were going to say that?" She put the car into gear and hit the gas, ready to risk it all.

SIXTEEN

Naomi raced down the stairwell, covering her face with her *kapp* and keeping it tucked into the crook of her elbow. Smoke already billowed around her as the flames spread fast in the old house from above. Somewhere, Jim Clark waited for his brother to return. The idea only added fuel to her own anger. Had he done the same for his brother eight years ago? Had he hung around in the downstairs of the coal mine manager's house knowing full well what Keith planned with her upstairs? Had he laughed with other partygoers while he waited to clean up his brother's crimes that night?

Just like he was tonight?

All this time, she thought he had innocently happened upon her outside by the trash container. Instead, he had been waiting for her there to clean up his brother's crime.

And tonight was no different.

All Naomi could do was press on and not let fear slow her down. Her time to face Jim would come, and God would be with her just as He had been with her upstairs with Jim's brother. There was no other reason for her escape than help from God. He stopped her killing just as He had stopped her car from falling any farther down the embankment when she was pushed off the road.

The rock that had stopped her car was used by God, the rock of her life.

If she would let Him be.

If she wanted Him to be.

She slid down each step with no one beside her, and yet surprisingly, she didn't feel alone.

Are you with me, Gott? *Have You always been with me? Even in my darkest and scariest times that began in this house eight years ago?*

When Naomi had thought God had left her, she had been wrong. If she had sought His direction that night, she would have realized she was the one who wasn't listening. She didn't listen before she left for the party, and she didn't listen after.

I'm listening now.

At the bottom floor, heat scorched her back, and her eyes burned with smoke and tears. It wouldn't be long before the flames burned through the floors and the blaze fell to the first floor. She turned an ear to any sounds, but also her heart to *Gott*'s direction. From now on, Naomi didn't want to make a move without Him.

She coughed. Even with her *kapp* over her mouth, the smoke seeped into her lungs. She tightened the seal over her lips as her lungs burned. She ducked her face and listened for any sounds to guide her away from danger.

For *Gott* to guide her.

A car door shut somewhere outside. She took one

step toward the sound and stopped. Naomi quickly prayed for wisdom, and she soon surmised that Jim must be outside. Had he noticed the fire upstairs yet? She believed the sound came from the back of the house, and Naomi lifted the glass in front of her as she made her way in the opposite direction. Each movement was slow but steady, but just as she reached the front of the house, Jim yelled into the back door.

"Keith!" His panicked voice carried through the building as the back door slammed and she heard him stomping inside in a rush. Naomi reached for the doorknob of the front door. It didn't budge. She gave it a quick shake and pull, but realized it was locked. Fumbling in the dark, her hand landed on the deadbolt. She turned it, then reached for the doorknob again.

"Where's my brother?" Jim spoke from behind. The lethal tone aimed her way stilled her hand. She knew just beyond the door was Keith's body on the walkway below the upstairs window. She had no choice but to open the door and attempt to escape, even if it meant she revealed the answer to Jim's question.

She swung it wide, but he reached her before she took one step outside. He grabbed her arm and swung her around. She raised her other hand with the glass shard to slice his cheek, but he stopped her short, barely an inch from his face.

With his hand grasping her wrist, and their eyes locked on each other, a sick and twisted grin grew on his face. He squeezed hard. Her arm shook as she used every ounce of muscle to break free from his hold.

He laughed and added more and more pressure until she thought her wrist would snap in two. She couldn't hold on much longer. Blood trickled down from the palm of her hand where the sharp edges of the glass punctured her skin. The metallic smell of her blood mixed with the acrid smell of smoke swirling around them.

"I see why my brother liked you," Jim sneered. "You're not like the other Amish girls. They would have cowered in fear by now."

He squeezed harder than ever. A whimper escaped her tight lips. She could take it no more and let the glass slip from her fingers.

It smashed on the floor between them, but she kept her gaze locked on Jim's face. Victory showed in his gleaming, beady eyes, but he didn't release her wrist. Instead, he squeezed harder until Naomi cried out in agonizing pain.

Her legs gave out beneath her as a fiery pain radiated from her wrist. Her knees buckled, and he brought her down to the floor to stand over her in a domineering pose.

He smirked. "You're a challenge, but Keith always likes a challenge."

Naomi breathed deep and let it out slowly. "Liked," she said. "Keith always *liked* a challenge."

Jim flinched and squinted. "Why?" The ceiling above splintered and pieces of flaming pieces of wood fell to the floor behind them. There was no going back the way they came. "What did you do?" He looked back at her in a panic.

She turned her head to look out to the walkway. The still body lying there proved Keith was done tormenting innocent young women and anyone else who caught his eye.

Suddenly, her wrist came free as Jim let her go. He ran out and down the steps to his brother, shouting, "Keith!" Anguish threaded his voice. He lifted his limp brother, smacking his face and listening for his breathing. He frantically searched for a pulse as Naomi slipped out the door. She wouldn't have another moment to escape.

"You!" Jim yelled her way as she reached the driveway. She saw his truck was pulled down to the back of the house. "You killed him!"

Naomi searched the long road that disappeared into blackness beyond the roaring flames of the house. The coal mine was down there off the road, as well as the entrance to the property. She remembered it being a long way from town with not many homes nearby. It was why the place made for a private locale for a teenage party. No one came out this far from town.

With no choice, she started toward the winding road. The land declined into a steep hill. It slowed her steps, and she locked her knees to keep from falling headfirst. She heard Jim's footsteps come up behind her in a pounding rush.

"Get back here!" he yelled. "You're not getting away with this!"

Naomi ran blindly down the hill, knowing she'd never escape his clutches but had to try. A few moments later, Jim slammed into her so hard, she flew forward. She hit the ground on a skid and started rolling.

Naomi screamed with pain from her fall. She cried

out in frantic fear at being caught. She saw no more hope of living for another day.

Jim reached her and flipped her over. She rose up on her hands and tried to scuttle back away from him, but with one quick jab, he punched her in the eye, sending her back to the ground grasping her face.

In the next second, Jim scooped her up and threw her over his shoulder.

Naomi kicked and hit his back as Jim walked farther down the road. She had no idea where they were going, but it wasn't long before she realized the destination.

The entrance to the mine had once been boarded up, but as he passed through the opening, she realized he had left earlier to open it.

"Why are we going in here?" she yelled.

He flung her off his shoulder and dropped her hard on the ground. The air from her lungs exited in a rush, and bright lights danced in her eyes on the impact.

"I should have brought you here eight years ago," he said. "If I had known you would kill my brother, I would have killed you then."

"I thought you weren't a killer," she replied, using his words.

"I'm not, but if accidents happen—oh, well." With that, he gave a swift kick to her stomach and left her there, grabbing hold of herself.

He returned to the opening and looked back. "I hope your death is painful as you run out of air." He stepped out and the door slammed behind him, sealing off all light and oxygen from the outside.

Naomi stretched her arm out to the door. "No, please, don't do this!" But it was too late. She was locked inside an old mine, and no one would ever know where to find her. Jim's brother might have taken her innocence, but Jim would take away her life. He'd steal everything from her. Her home, her family and now her future with the man she loved.

Sheriff Shaw gave orders for all emergency personnel to be dispatched to the coal mine. In a town with only one ambulance, and that bus already in use with the officer down, she was relying on the firemen to handle the paramedics' job.

"You're expecting the worst," Sawyer said to her as she raced her cruiser toward the smoke billowing in the sky. "You know she's there."

"I have to plan for all scenarios. It's my job to expect the worst." She looked his way, the flashing lights of the other cruisers casting a red glare on her face. "But I never stop hoping. And don't you either."

Sawyer faced forward to watch the angry billows reaching high up to the stars. He didn't see any flames, but the smoke was what would kill first. He pushed the thoughts from his mind and silently prayed for *Gott* to give her air to breathe. He didn't know what that would look like, but he knew *Gott* would find a way. He felt the stirrings of hope just thinking of His almighty power.

"I don't think I ever lost hope." Sawyer blurted out the confession weighing on his heart. "A part of me always believed there was more to the story. That I didn't have all the facts, even as I listened to what my family said about Naomi choosing the English lifestyle over ours. I never once fully accepted what I was told. And

Liza never did either. Maybe that was why I needed to be around her. She was the only person who never stopped hoping and believing in Naomi." Tears sprang to his eyes. "Liza died never knowing she was right."

Cassie's lips curved into a serene smile. "That's the wonderful thing about belief. When you truly believe, you don't need validation from other people. You already know it in your heart."

Sawyer smiled, thinking of his wife's words she lived by. *My heart wants what* Gott *says.* He nodded and whispered, "*Ya*, she did."

"I have to think she would be happy for you."

"About what?" Sawyer glanced her way, confused at such a statement.

She took the turn up to the coal mine. "I'm sorry if I am breaking your code or rules about personal things, and if I've gone too far, just tell me and I'll stop, but I believe Liza wanted you to keep on believing. I think she would be happy for you…and Naomi." The last part was said in a whisper, but it blared in Sawyer's ears.

"I loved my wife," he said quickly. "I truly did. I miss her daily. But I…"

The smoking house came into view as the car curved up and around the hill. Flames burst from all the windows, a menacing sight of creeping tentacles.

"I can't lose Naomi." He blurted out the confession from deep within him. "Is it possible to love two people?"

Cassie stopped her car and threw open the door. She jumped out, and turned back to say, "I'd say so, since you do. Stay here." She slammed the door on Sawyer.

He sat stunned at her words, though she only told him what he always knew.

He would always love Naomi. He always did.

But he also loved Liza and always would.

He laughed at the ludicrousness of such a thought. The only person who would understand would be Liza. She would know not to listen to what her mind said. That this was a thought for her heart. What would her heart say?

Go get Naomi. She needs you.

That was what it would say.

Sawyer grabbed at his chest, scrunching his blue shirt in his gripping fingers. The thought had been loud and clear. It went against Cassie's orders. It went against logic for him to even approach a flaming house unprotected and short on knowledge. Only the firemen should even try.

Sawyer opened the passenger door and stepped out. Warnings filled his mind. As he walked past a cluster of people hovering together, he kept his face to the fire. He approached the house, even while everything in his brain told him to go back to the car. *You'll die. You'll endanger others.* The thoughts kept coming with each footstep. But when he reached the front steps, the flames flicked at him to stop him from going any farther. The door was open where the firefighters had gone in already.

Sawyer turned in the safest direction and followed a broken concrete walkway that led around the house. Each step he took was blind, but sure. Quickly, he picked up his pace until he'd made it around to the back of the house.

Then he heard the sound of a car door slam somewhere through the trees. He tilted an ear to determine any other sounds.

"Think with my heart by following *Gott*'s lead," he said to himself. He turned away from the house and walked down the hill. When he stood in the thick of the trees, he scanned around him, down low and up high. He stepped to his right, around a tree trunk, and his boot hit something.

The land plateaued ahead, and he could see beyond the drop-off. He moved forward and reached the edge of the plateau. That was when he saw the outline of a person walking away from a truck.

Jim's truck.

But the outline of the man looked to be carrying someone. The way the legs and head dangled told Sawyer the person was not awake. Possibly already dead.

"Stop right there!" he shouted, already slipping down the hill.

The figure halted and slowly turned to face him. "You're too late!"

He recognized the voice. It was Jim Clark who shouted back, anger bursting from his voice.

Sawyer froze. *He was too late?*

He dropped his gaze at the body in Jim's arms. Could he look at her? Could he face the fact that this time, Naomi wasn't alive and well? That she never would be again?

All because of this man.

Sawyer lifted his face to the man who had befriended him. The man who had infiltrated his life to make sure he never went after Naomi. "That's what this was all about, wasn't it? Everything you did, you did to make sure I never found her."

"I did it all to protect him, and I would do it all again," Jim said, his voice almost maniacal.

Him?

Sawyer thought maybe he had heard wrong. He took a few slow steps forward. "Do you mean you sent Naomi away to protect her attacker?" A few more steps, and Jim's shadowy figure began to show his features.

Still Sawyer kept his gaze on Jim, not ready to see Naomi's lifeless body.

"He made one mistake. He was young. Could you imagine what would have happened to him when the press found out?"

"That man did not make a mistake. He knew exactly what he was doing, and *Gott* will be his judge."

Jim burst out with a loud scream, lifting the body up, then dropping to his knees with it. Sawyer rushed forward to stop him from falling on Naomi.

Only a few more steps, and Sawyer realized Jim wasn't holding Naomi.

He was holding a man.

A dead man.

"Jim, who is this?" Sawyer demanded, racing faster up to the man who had been a friend for eight years.

"My brother. My little brother," Jim wailed, but Sawyer couldn't give him a moment of compassion.

"Jim, where is Naomi?" Sawyer looked around. To one side was the entrance to the old mine. To the other was the billowing smoke and the now fully engulfed house. "Where is Naomi?" he demanded again, his voice in a rising panic. Had she been in the house the whole time?

"Where I should have put her eight years ago when I found her by the trash," Jim sneered and looked toward the mine. "Now I know she'll never tell again."

SEVENTEEN

Jim Clark didn't think he was a killer. He saw himself as a protector. He truly believed all he did for his brother was what he was supposed to do. It didn't matter that a whole community of Amish people were hurt in the process. It didn't matter that lives were ripped apart. It didn't matter that two women died.

And she would be next.

Naomi groaned in pain. Her right eye had already sealed shut where he had punched her to force her to comply.

Would anyone find her now?

Naomi thought of the innocent baby in all of this. Chloe had been left an orphan and would now lose her too. "Protect her, please, *Gott*." Naomi didn't hold out any hope of being found in this dark tunnel. No one had been here since the place shut down ten years ago. Why would they come now? Especially for an ex-Amish woman nobody wanted around anyway.

Naomi had come back to Rogues Ridge to protect Chloe. She knew driving into this town, her community would reject her. But she had hoped they would welcome a baby in need of help.

She still held on to that hope.

For Chloe.

All Naomi had wanted was to protect her. She'd even been willing to face rejection again to be sure the child was safe. She would have done anything for her. Naomi was surprised Jim Clark hadn't understood that drive in her. Nothing he tried, not even shooting her, scared her away. He was willing to kill for his brother in order to protect his reputation. How could he not see that also made him a killer? How could he not see his protection of his brother only hurt more and more people?

She pushed up on her elbows in the cold dirt. Sharp rocks bit into the flesh of her arms. She looked out her one opened eye in the direction of the tightly sealed door but had no more strength to crawl over to it.

Calling out was impossible. Her throat would make no sounds in her raw voice. And no one would hear her, even if the authorities arrived for the fire. They wouldn't even know to come looking for her. She was running out of the thin oxygen with each of her breaths.

Her elbows gave out, and she fell facedown. Her body could take no more. It was a night of toxic smoke inhaled in her lungs, and now, limited oxygen when she needed it most. Death drew near.

Naomi's cheek rested in the dirt, and her mouth remained open to take whatever air she could catch. Her one good eye drifted closed with the other, and she had no more strength to open them again.

The flashlights' beams bounced off the walls of a narrow tunnel. Sawyer walked alongside Cassie and had his own light. She'd given it to him after the officers had descended down on Jim.

The man hadn't gone quietly, but he also hadn't put up a fight. His devoted life to his younger brother had already broken him and destroyed his mind. Sawyer prayed he would find peace. Then he'd quickly run to the mine and started heaving the rocks that blocked the door from opening. He'd had it open before the sheriff joined him.

"She's up ahead," Cassie announced, her light revealing a small frame against the tunnel wall. His light fell on the small heap that was Naomi. He ran to her, falling on his knees and rolling her over. Her limp body felt as if it had no life left in it.

"Naomi, I'm here, *liebe*. I came for you." He willed her to hear him. That somehow she was still in there.

"Step back," a fireman instructed him, but Sawyer only moved to sit up by her head. He touched her matted curls and rubbed her still face. With all flashlights on her, he could see she wasn't breathing.

A neighboring town brought the fire department their ambulance with lifesaving equipment, but as he held Naomi's lifeless head, he wondered if any of it would help.

The workings of the professionals blurred before him as they connected Naomi to machines and an oxygen mask to get her lungs to work again. They moved her to a stretcher and lifted her up to roll her out to the ambulance waiting by the door.

Time raced by and soon she was lifted up inside and the doors closed on her. Sawyer was left to stand alone as the ambulance raced away with its sirens on.

He remembered the same deserted feeling when Liza had passed away. It was the same feeling he'd had when Naomi left town, as well.

And now he was left behind again.

His life would always be one of solitude. Sawyer shoved his hands in his pockets and started to walk back up the hill, but just before he reached the plateau, someone called his name from behind.

Cassie stood at the bottom of the hill. "If you're coming with me to the hospital, we need to go now."

"To be told she was dead before she arrived?" Sawyer said.

Cassie nodded. "If that's the message, yes. But it should be told to someone who loved her. Don't you think she deserved that? Not to die alone?"

Sawyer realized his selfishness in an instant. He was thinking only of his own feelings of solitude, when he had more time to hope for more. Naomi didn't. But there were others who needed to be there for her too.

"We need to stop at her parents' house." He took the steps down the hill, more determined to do right by Naomi. "They should be there. They loved her too."

At Cassie's nod, they set out to make the stop and pick up the Kemps. It was a silent group who entered the emergency room doors and approached the desk. Hours later, all four were ushered into the intensive care area, where they were directed to Naomi's bed behind a wall of glass.

She hadn't died on the way, but she wasn't living on her own either.

The machines around her beeped and kept her alive. Sawyer remembered Liza in her last days, and how he had sat bedside holding her hand into death. He took a chair now and brought it to Naomi's right side. He sat and filled his hands with her limp one.

Her parents did the same on Naomi's left side. Her *mamm* wept softly and stroked Naomi's curls from her face like Naomi did so many times to tame them. A metaphor for her life. No matter how hard she tried to be the best Amish girl, her wildness came out. It made her feel alone, seeking the approval of others. Even a bunch of English high schoolers. The idea of Naomi never waking to find out she was never alone to begin with cut Sawyer to the bone.

But that wasn't what hurt the most.

The idea of Naomi never waking and no longer being in his life was what stole his breath from his lungs.

It was saying goodbye forever that would hurt the most.

EIGHTEEN

The melodious song lifted from a chorus, or so it seemed. It was a song of joy, yet it wasn't loud or rambunctious. Instead, the tune remained low and sweet, and it eased her breathing to a steady rhythm and reminded her of the songs her Amish community sang while they worked. The hymn sounded so close, and she yearned to sing along, but her lungs felt so tight.

Slowly, air filtered in, and it felt good to breathe. She filled her lungs deeper this time and let her breath out slowly. Then she did it again.

The singing stopped, followed by silence, but she still took another breath.

"She's breathing."

She heard the voice and recognized it. Her *mamm* speaking from someplace close by. Naomi felt something squeeze her hands.

She squeezed back.

"Oh, Naomi! Come back to us!" Her *mamm*'s sweet voice filled her ears. But how could that be? This had to be a dream…or maybe she died.

"Don't rush her. We just took her off the machines."

"Daed?" Naomi rasped out at hearing her father's voice. Were they real? Or was this a part of her imagination?

"Yes, dear, we're all here. Your *mamm* and the bishop and a whole slew of friends for certain sure. Take your time. We've got the rest of our lives." His voice hitched on that last part as though tears choked his words. "Thank You, *Gott*, for second chances."

His words calmed her. She didn't understand why they were there, or if it was even true, but in the moment, she was thankful for their presence.

Then she opened her eyes as she remembered what happened. "Chloe!" she choked out, and her voice was unrecognizable. A beeping sound pulsed fast and blared in a dim room as she searched the faces around a bed.

Her bed.

People she never thought would sit vigil for her, alive or dead, stood around her with expectant faces.

Her chorus, who had sung her awake.

Frantically, she looked for the one who could answer the only question she wanted answered. *Where was Chloe?*

Her right hand was squeezed. "Chloe is alive and well. Just like you." She could hear the smile in his voice, but something blocked her right eye and her view of him.

Slowly, Naomi moved her head so she could see out her left eye. "Sawyer."

"I'm right beside you."

"He's been here the whole time," Bishop Bontrager said from the end of the bed. His white beard bobbed with a joyful grin. The doctor and a nurse stood on either side of him with smiles. "Never stopped believing," the bishop said.

Sawyer frowned. "I learned my lesson from eight years ago. I won't ever doubt you again."

Naomi thought this whole scene had to be a dream. She was the one who needed to repent. She looked around the room, first at her parents, then at the bishop. When they knew the truth of her assault, they would leave for certain sure, as they would say in their Amish way of speaking. The thought that they already knew caused her heart to jump a few beats. She turned her head back to Sawyer but caught Anna and Esau by the door. The couple stood together, but Anna's straight face proved that this wasn't a dream. All these people were really here, and Anna didn't hide her rejection like the rest did.

If they all knew, then they were being kind for the moment.

"Sawyer," she whispered and pulled his hand close.

"What is it, *liebe*?" He leaned down and turned an ear to her lips.

"Did you tell them? Do they know?" Her questions were barely a whisper, only for his ear to hear.

He shook his head against her and whispered back, "I would never think of doing such a thing." He straightened back up and said louder, "But every person in this room respects your reason for leaving, with no questions asked."

Naomi couldn't fathom such a statement. She knew they could require a penance from her. "How?" she rasped.

Bishop Bontrager smiled warmly. "Sometimes, we

don't need to know the details. Sometimes, we just need to celebrate that one of our own has returned home, where she always belonged."

Tears sprang to Naomi's eyes and blurred her already compromised vision. "Why can't I see?"

"Oh, that will come with time," Bishop Bontrager said. "We just want you to get your strength back and come back to us when you're ready. But if you ever do want to share, please know you can. I will listen with no judgment. Just listen."

Naomi's heart swelled at this man's leadership. The rest of the community would follow his lead. Hope for returning to the Amish took solid root. "Thank you, Bishop. I am so thankful." She swallowed and cringed at the pain in her throat. She looked to Sawyer and said, "But I was asking why can't I see with my eyes? Something's blocking me."

Dead silence ensued.

Then Bishop Bontrager let out a robust laugh. She didn't think she had ever seen him so relaxed. His eyes actually twinkled. "You're wearing a bandage over your eye, dear. Your eye was injured. But regardless, my answer remains the same. I'm here to listen anytime." He looked around and said, "Why don't we give Naomi some time to rest?"

Slowly, people turned to leave the room, and both *Mamm* and Sawyer released her hands to join them.

"Not you, son," Bishop Bontrager. "I think you might have something to ask Naomi, *ya*?"

Sawyer's eyes widened and his face flushed. He looked to Naomi and back to the bishop. "*Ya*, if it's possible. I would really like to do that, Bishop."

Bishop Bontrager looked pleased. He nodded and said, "I'll leave you two to your…discussion." He winked and exited with the rest of the people milling about on the other side of the glass wall.

Sawyer sat on the edge of the bed with his back to the glass. He didn't say anything at first, and Naomi waited expectantly for whatever he needed to ask her.

"They're all watching, aren't they?" he asked.

Naomi looked behind him and saw a cluster of people peering in at them. They quickly glanced to the ceiling and pretended to be busy. Naomi bit back a smile and nodded to Sawyer, whose flushed face was redder than before.

"Are you well?" she asked.

"I will be in a moment. I hope so anyway. I hope all will be well." He retook her hand and held her gently. He swallowed so hard, she heard him gulp. "First, I need you to know that I loved Liza."

Naomi inhaled sharply. She wasn't expecting him to say that but realized how appropriate it was. "I know," she said.

"I'm sorry if that upsets you, but—"

"Not at all. I loved Liza too. She will always have a place in my heart."

Sawyer smiled on a sigh. "Me too." He cleared his throat. "Having said that, I also want you to know losing you was so painful. I didn't know how to go on. I wanted to be near Liza just so I could be close to you. Both of us found healing being friends, and after three years of friendship, I asked her to marry me."

"Sawyer, you don't need to tell me this," Naomi whispered.

"I want nothing to come between us this time."

"This time?"

"It's my hope that you'll return to the Amish," Sawyer blurted out. He chewed on his lower lip as his nerves took over.

"Oh," she said, a little let down that that was what he wanted to say. "If I am able, I would like that very much. Thank you."

"That's not all I wanted to say. You see, the truth is… The truth is…"

"The truth is hard," she said. "Sometimes knowing it means you stand alone," she repeated her words to him from before. "But sometimes knowing it can also mean you find the people you are supposed to stand with."

His shoulders dropped into a relaxed pose. "The truth is I've always loved you, Naomi. I've never stopped, and I would like you to finally give me your answer to my proposal. I'd like to be your *mann* forever. If you'll have me."

Tears sprang to her eyes, and she wanted to rip the bandage off so she could see him clearly. Instead, she reached for his cheek and brought him closer. "Leaving you was the hardest thing I ever did. It never stopped hurting, and I never stopped loving you either. My answer was going to be yes."

"And is it still a yes? I will be your *mann*?"

"*Ya*, and I will be your *fraa*."

They simultaneously whispered "Forever" as Sawyer leaned in to place a sweet kiss on her lips. She reached for his face to hold on, never wanting to be apart from Sawyer Zook again.

In the next moment, they heard claps and cheers

from the other side of the window. Everyone seemed happy about a wedding coming up soon, a wedding they had expected eight years ago. Now it was finally coming to pass.

Sawyer pulled back slightly, meeting her gaze with bright, happy eyes. "I think they approve."

"Is it weird that I wish Liza was here?" Naomi said in all seriousness.

His smile fell, but for only a moment. He shook his head and laughed. Tears filled his eyes as he said, "Not at all. She would have loved this. She loved you so much. She loved us both with her whole heart."

Naomi met his teary gaze with her own wet eyes. "She was always good about following her heart. Something I am trying to do more of. Like right now." She leaned up and kissed Sawyer quickly on the lips.

A knock came on the opened door, and Sawyer stood up so they could see who was entering.

The sheriff walked in with Chloe in her arms. "Look who's up, Chloe," Cassie said in a sweet tone. "It's your mama."

Chloe smiled bright, the recent events seeming to leave her untouched.

Naomi reached a hand to the baby, then realized what Cassie just said. "I haven't let her know me as that. I've only referred to myself as Naomi with her."

Cassie brought the baby to the bedside. "I understand. But here's the thing. Chloe doesn't have a mother. She also doesn't have any next of kin. Debby was in the foster system and was never adopted. So, you're the closest thing Chloe has to a mom, and I would like to know before the state finds her a foster home if you would like to be considered. And by considered, I mean chosen." Cassie waggled her eyebrows at Naomi. "What do you say?"

Naomi was sure she had stopped breathing. She glanced out the glass partition at her parents, then up at Sawyer. No one gave her any kind of signal or direction.

"I know what I want to do," she said. "But, Sawyer, if we're going to be married, you should have a say in this. What do you think?"

"Well, I know what my head says."

"What's that?" she asked.

"That I already think she's my child." He smiled and scooped Chloe up in his arms from Cassie's.

"And your heart?" Naomi asked.

"My heart already loves her." He kissed Chloe's cheek.

Naomi beamed at the sight. "And *Gott*? What does He say?"

A voice cleared from the doorway that pulled their attention to the door and ceased the conversation.

Anna stood on the threshold. Her clothes were perfectly pressed and proper, and her face was still void of a smile. "I know what *Gott* says," she said.

Naomi warily asked, "What's that, Anna?"

"He says that children are a heritage from Him. Chloe would be blessed to have you both as parents."

Naomi looked up at Sawyer to find him beaming at his sister. "Thank you, Anna, for saying such a kind thing."

Anna nodded and looked at Naomi. "My *brudder* loves you very much. I only wanted to protect his heart from breaking again."

Naomi reached for Sawyer's hand. "Because I know the pain, you can be certain sure I won't break it again."

Anna's eyes closed, and when she opened them again, a smile cracked her lips. A smile for Naomi alone. She backed out of the room quickly, leaving Cassie to discuss the next steps to adoption. It would be a long road with all the legalities, but no matter what hurdles they had to face, it would be worth it. Chloe would be worth it.

Suddenly, Naomi, Sawyer and Chloe found themselves alone as people gave the soon-to-be family some time to celebrate the next journey of their lives.

"I never thought coming home would be like this. I never would have dared to dream it could be this wonderful," Naomi said, cuddling with Chloe on the bed.

"It's beyond my imagination too," Sawyer said, leaning down to brush the baby's auburn curls, which were growing fast. "We will do Debby proud."

Naomi smiled. "I will make sure Chloe will always know she had a wonderful mother who gave her a chance at life." She kissed Chloe's forehead, then reached for Sawyer's hand to connect their little family. "And how *Gott* gave us all a second chance together."

* * * * *

If you enjoyed this story, look for
Amish Country Undercover *by Katy Lee*
from Love Inspired Suspense.

Dear Reader,

I am so thrilled to be able to tell you another Rogues Ridge, Kentucky, story. Naomi and Sawyer faced a lot of hurdles before their paths brought them back together for the purpose of protecting an innocent life. Little Chloe was a joy to write, and I hope you fell in love with this beautiful family.

Adoption is a beautiful thing, and it is near to my heart. My husband and I had the blessing of fostering and adopting, so I know firsthand how someone can bring hope to an innocent child in need of a loving home and family. Naomi and Sawyer gave Chloe a chance at life, and that showed through in their selfless choices to do everything they could to keep her safe. They will have a wonderful home, filled with love and contagious laughter.

Thank you all for reading! I love to connect with readers. You can find me on Facebook and Instagram. Or contact me through my website, www.katyleebooks.com.

Blessings,
Katy Lee